FORGIVEN! REDEEMED! RECONCILED!

Stories of Prodigals

Dorsey Burk

ARPress
ILLUMINATING IDEAS
EMPOWERING VOICES

ARPress
45 Dan Road Suite 5
Canton MA 02021

Hotline: 1(888) 821-0229
Fax: 1(508) 545-7580

Ordering Information:

Quantity sales. Special discounts are available on quantity purchases by corporations, associations, and others. For details, contact the publisher at the address above.

Printed in the United States of America.

ISBN-13:   Paperback   979-8-89676-045-0
                eBook   979-8-89676-046-7

Library of Congress Control Number: 2025900540

Contents

The Prodigal Father

DEDICATION

To Abigayle, Rebekka, Alexis, Crysellyn, Javan, Samara, Kaidyn, Rosalie, and Avianna because we all need forgiveness, redemption, and reconciliation.

The Prodigal Husband

CHAPTER 1
Wednesday, July 31, 2058

The sanctuary was beautiful. Twenty-three large floral sprays and arrangements adorned the steps leading to the platform. Interspersed among them were thirty-inch-square photos highlighting aspects of a busy life: acting in a skit before her middle school students, changing a baby's diaper in the church nursery, speaking at a ladies' conference in Zambia, washing an elephant at the elephant orphanage in Sri Lanka, kneeling in prayer, eating with her family at McDonald's, making peanut brittle for a youth fundraiser, embracing a young woman while imparting wisdom to her.

Alone in the sanctuary, except for an usher at the rear doors, and dressed in his new charcoal suit with a new bright, paisley silk tie, Zachery Zane Petersen raised his hands in worship as he stood in front of his wife's flower-draped casket. As tears rolled down his cheeks, he thanked the Lord for a life well lived and for the blessing his wife had been to him. He prayed for strength to make it through the time of visitation and then the memorial service that would follow. As he prayed, his daughters Sara and Sophie quietly slipped their arms around his waist and hugged him. Zach smiled and said, "It's time. Let's do this. Let's celebrate her life!" He then nodded to the usher to open the double doors.

Even though a record heat wave blanketed the city, Zach was pleasantly surprised by the mass of people waiting to express their sympathy and to share anecdotes with the family. Even three hours later, the line stretched down the aisle, through the doors, and into the foyer. Many were still in line when the funeral director asked the people to be seated so the service could begin.

A few minutes later, he sat in the middle of the first row in the center section of the church auditorium, between Sara, his older daughter, and Sophie, his younger daughter. Surrounded by family, he kept a tight rein on his emotions. He was delighted that the service was going as he had planned. The video clip and music were powerful. Several speakers told of the impact Kara Petersen had made on their lives by a tender embrace, a word fitly spoken, or a freshly baked pie. However, Zach just had to release his emotions as the chorale sang Richard Smallwood's "Total Praise." He just couldn't remain seated; he stood and freely praised God through his tears. Then one of Kara's long-time mentors eulogized his wife. His wife would have loved the service. It was befitting her extraordinary life.

But their early years were far from idyllic.

CHAPTER 2

Thursday, March 2, 2017

Zach was euphoric. He was thrilled that the shortened business session had allowed the ministerial conference to end a day early. He couldn't wait to get home. He had checked out of the hotel and stowed his bags in his SUV before the final workshop this morning. He would drive part of the way home today and surprise Kara early tomorrow afternoon. She would be so pleased that he had been elected state youth secretary. He would take her to her favorite restaurant to celebrate.

Light snow hampered the last part of the drive home, but Zach was used to driving in wintery weather. After all, even though he no longer lived in the state, he was a Minnesotan through and through and well trained to drive on ice and snow. His car didn't even slide one time. Neither did the weather dampen his spirits.

Zach was surprised to see his twin's car parked on the street as he pulled into the garage. He grabbed his bags and slipped into the kitchen. It was immaculate as always. Zach was proud that he always knew unexpected guests would always find a clean home. He mounted the stairs and opened the door of the master bedroom.

His bags fell to the floor as he saw his wife in her panties and bra while his brother was in only his boxers. His brother paled as his wife shrieked. Zach turned and ran from the house. His tires squealed as he backed out of the garage and onto the street. He got back on the freeway and headed west. He didn't care where he went. He just had to get away from what he had just witnessed.

He raced down the interstate, weaving in and out of traffic, as if putting distance between him and his home would change the image burned on his mind. Eventually as he gained more control over his emotions, Zach exited the freeway and aimlessly meandered the country roads, trying to understand how his marriage and ministry could really be over. Then he saw the beckoning neon lights of a bar.

He returned home shortly after midnight and parked in the driveway. Anger coursed through him as he saw Geoff's car still in front of his house. Anna, Geoff's wife, had parked her car on the street too. Bracing for whatever he might face, Zach entered the front door. Kara, Geoff, and Anna were sitting in the living room. Red eyes and gentle sobs greeted him. He glared at the trio. Anger as he had never known surged through him. He didn't realize he had even moved until he heard the bone break and saw the blood gush from Geoff's nose as pain shot up his own arm. Geoff disarmed him as he quietly said, "I deserve that. I'm sorry, Zach!"

Kara, curled up in the corner of the sofa, pleaded, "Zach, it's not what you think! I love you!"

Zach turned to her. The fury and hurt in Zach's eyes nailed her to the sofa. Kara had never seen him like this. She shrank as if he might attack her, although she had only felt love and security in his embrace. "Yeah, I saw how much you love me. I thought we had something special." Then he turned to Anna. "What are you doing here? Am I the only one not invited for a threesome?"

Anna shot out of her chair and slapped Zach across his face. "How dare you!" she yelled. "You don't even know what's going on."

"It's quite evident what's going on! It doesn't take a Ph.D. to know what's going on when a husband finds his wife in her panties and bra in the bedroom with another man dressed only in skivvies. My own twin brother! Don't tell me I don't know what's going on! I saw!" Zack screamed. "Your being here, Anna, only shows that you condone or even participated in this. The only question is how long has this been going on? How long have I been played the fool?" Tears ran down Zack's cheeks.

Shaking from anger, Zach took a deep breath. He looked each of them in the eye and said quietly but succinctly through clenched teeth, "This is my home. I want ALL of you out of here NOW! Take her to your own bedroom, brother! I'm sure three can fit nicely in your king bed."

Sobs escaped as Kara sunk down in the sofa at those words. With a towel at his nose, Geoff said, "I'm not leaving until we explained what happened."

"I don't need your explanation! I know what I saw!" Zach said as he crumbled to the floor and burst into gut-wrenching groans as tears wet the carpet. "Please, just leave."

"It's not what you think, Zach! Nothing happened. We were doing it for you!" Geoff said.

"You were doing it for me, but nothing happened. Get out! All three of you. NOW!"

"Zach, please listen to them," Anna pleaded, trying to fix the situation.

"OUT! NOW! Thank God we don't have any kids!" Zach screamed.

A new round of sobs escaped Kara's throat as Zach stumbled down the hallway and slammed the master bedroom's door.

CHAPTER 3
Sunday, March 5, 2017

The Reverend Richard S. Tanner opened the door to his home. "Zach, you look horrible! I knew something had to be terribly wrong for you to ask to speak to me on a Sunday morning, especially without notice and when we both had church. What happened? Let's go to my office and you can tell me."

Zach slipped into the chair offered him and said, "Thanks, Uncle Rick, for meeting me this morning. I'm sorry you had to cancel a preaching engagement to make this happen. I just told my assistant that he would have to take over this morning without explaining anything to him. However, you were the only one I could think of that could help. I didn't know who else to turn to. I need you to be a friend today. Not my favorite uncle or my district superintendent. I need you to tell me what to do. An *incident* occurred Friday that has left me an emotional, spiritual, and mental wreck. Oh, I wish I could forget the past three days!"

Haltingly, Zach described what happened Friday afternoon. "I was so stoked after the conference. My election as the district youth secretary was a total surprise. I didn't see it coming at all. What a great twenty-seventh birthday gift. I was so happy and yet humbled as I drove home. I knew Kara would be thrilled. I was so glad that I could surprise her by coming home Friday afternoon instead of Saturday." Tears began to mar Zach's face.

"I was euphoric when I got home! Then, pardon the expression, all hell broke loose. I got home a day earlier than Kara expected. I quietly slipped into the kitchen and quietly climbed the stairs as I wanted to surprise her. I grabbed the door handle and opened our bedroom door. My bags fell to the floor when I saw Kara and Geoff standing in front of the dresser. She was in her panties and bra. Geoff was in his boxers. He had one hand was on her waist and the other on her shoulder. Their street clothes were folded on the vanity chair. I have never been more shocked in my life or more devastated! I couldn't believe what I saw. My wife and my twin brother standing in their underwear in my bedroom! The pain was unreal! I dropped my suitcases, ran out of the house, and jumped in the car. I just drove for hours. Hours!

"It didn't matter where I went. I just had to get away. I was so angry! All I could think about was my marriage was over, so my ministry was too. Everything I've worked for was gone. I felt so totally helpless. Why did God let this happen?

"Uncle Rick, I later pulled off the interstate and roamed country roads. There was nothing in sight except farmland and a few homes and barns. Eventually I came to an intersection of two country highways. The neon lights of a bar caught my attention. It was the only building in sight. Since my life as I knew it was over, I pulled into the parking lot and killed the engine. I just wanted to blot out what I had seen. Uncle Rick, the only alcohol I've ever tasted in my life was once when real wine was used for communion instead of grape juice at a church I was visiting.

"Anyway, I opened the car door to step out. As I put my left foot on the ground, the door slammed against my shin, awakening me to my surroundings. Immediately, I felt the gentle hands of Jesus enfolding me. I just sat in front of that bar and repented for what I almost had done and wept and cried and wept some more. The love of God was so overwhelming! Just like when the father ran to his prodigal son. Except in this case, I was the prodigal husband.

"I pulled into our driveway about 12:30. I had been driving aimlessly for over seven hours. When I went home both Geoff and Anna were in the family room with Kara. I lost it again! Worse this time! Without realizing it, I slugged Geoff, breaking his nose.

"After some words I'm ashamed of, I told them all three to leave.

I crumbled to the floor as sobs tore through my body. I pulled myself up, took enough Tylenol PM to make me sleep, and went on to bed. I'm surprised I didn't take the whole bottle. I slept through Saturday, again thanks to the Tylenol PM, and only got up in time to shower and come here.

"About 4:00 Saturday morning, I got up to use the toilet. Geoff heard me and forced me to go to the family room and listen to them!

"God, I don't know what to do! You must help me, Lord!" Zach prayed.

With tears streaming, Zach continued, "They told me—it's a nightmare I can't believe—that Anna had the idea that Geoff could impregnant Kara, and they would pretend it was my baby. We've been married almost seven years and haven't gotten pregnant one time. When I had my motorcycle accident my first year of college—I think you remember—the impact fractured my pelvis in several places and damaged—uh—some other parts. Almost in passing, the orthopedic doctor said the pelvis would heal but the other damage might cause infertility issues. After seven years without Kara getting pregnant, I admit that I've been concerned, but not to the point of going to a urologist or a fertility specialist.

"Uncle Rick, what do I do? I'm a pastor. Kara's a pastor's wife. Geoff and Anna are key leaders in our church. I got home before anything intimate happened. BUT my God!—that's prayer, not a curse—I don't know what to do! If I had been a couple of hours later, they would have had sex. My twin brother and my wife! Regardless of their reason— regardless of how noble they thought it might be—it was wrong! How can I trust either one again? How can I go on as pastor after stopping at a bar to get drunk? How can I let Geoff and Anna lead ministries in my church?

"I'm devastated! I don't see any future. It feels like I'm a prodigal who's thrown everything away—when it really wasn't even my fault. I'm so glad we don't have any kids now, because I don't know if our marriage will survive. I prayed and prayed that God would send me the wife that He wanted me to have, one that would share my ministry and help me build a strong, dynamic church. I was sure Kara was the one! Was I wrong in marrying Kara?

"What do I do, Uncle Rick? I am so angry! I don't think I can face going back to the church. I feel so guilty. I almost got drunk. My wife almost committed adultery with my brother. My twin brother! But I don't have any markable skills. My degree in theology isn't worth much in a secular world. I'm not an accountant or contractor or doctor. Kara hasn't taught school since shortly after we married. She's been a pastor's wife. How do you put that on a resume? She couldn't survive financially if I divorce her.

"I love her! At least I want to. Geoff and I have always been so close, but I don't know if I can forgive him. I just don't know what to do," Zach cried. "I was so consumed with rage—with hate! Now it's just a deep, deep ache like I've never known. I just want to curl up in a ball and forget it all. Is there still hope for me in the ministry if I can keep the marriage together? If not, you can have my ministerial card now. I'll do whatever you suggest. I have never been so defeated, so broken, so directionless in my life. My life is in your hands. Tell me what to do."

CHAPTER 4
Sunday, March 5, 2017

Rick Tanner took a deep breath. Tears fill his eyes as he looked at Zach. "You said you didn't come for me to be your uncle or your ministerial elder but a friend. I think my advice would be different in each situation. First and foremost, let's pray.

Rick clasped Zach's hands in his and began to pray. "Heavenly Father, there is no one like You. You are our creator and redeemer, our savior. We honor You, Lord. We exalt You, Lord. We acknowledge that we desperately need Your wisdom and counsel. I see how broken Zach is. He feels betrayed by those closest to him. Heal his broken heart. Restore his strength. Give him wisdom to know and to follow Your will. Jesus, let the gifts of a word of wisdom and a word of knowledge flow through me as I try to help him. And Lord, we pray that you would help Kara, Geoff, and Anna. Renew your Spirit in them. In grace and mercy, restore them. Let them feel Your Spirit again as a living reality in their lives. We ask this in the name of Jesus Christ. Amen!"

Rick continued to hold Zach's hands and looked deep into his eyes. He finally said, "Zach, it hard for me to believe the story you just told me. It hard to wrap my mind around it. I've known you and Geoff all your lives and Kara and Anna almost as long. Even though you and Geoff lived in Sri Lanka, I've watched the four of you grow and mature as teens. You and Geoff even lived with us for a couple of summers. I've seen how the four of you dedicated your lives to Christ. I participated in both weddings. If I'm shocked by this, I know you are devastated!

"But, Zack, you've done nothing that is not forgivable by God. The emotional high you were on as you entered your house was shattered by what you consider betrayal. You fell instantly from a heady high to rock bottom and reacted humanly. At least you didn't use your gun. As far as the bar, Satan saw you at your weakest and tempted you. You won that battle.

"Now you're going to be facing the real battle. How you react to Kara, Geoff, and Anna is your choice. You can hate them and let bitterness destroy you. Bitterness will destroy your marriage—whether you divorce or not—and shatter family relationships. Or you can *choose* to forgive them. You can *choose* to love them. Forgiving and loving them will result in stronger relationships and a healthier marriage.

"Zack, as your friend, I'm asking do you love Kara? Can you forgive her? Can you love Geoff and Anna and forgive them?...Don't answer those questions now; I know you can't on your own. Love is a commitment, Zack. Better questions are: Are you *willing* to love them as Jesus loves them? Are you *willing* to let His love flow through you to them? Are you *willing* to humble yourself and let His wisdom and goodness lead you?"

Zach sat quietly for a few minutes and then lifted his red eyes to Rick. "I don't know! I want to! I want to love Kara; she's been my life. I want to love Geoff and Anna. But it couldn't hurt any more if they had ripped my heart out. They destroyed my trust. How can I ever believe them again? How can I ever have faith in them again? In some ways it seems like Kara's the prodigal wife who threw everything away and I'm the husband waiting at home. I want to run to her and embrace her and forgive her. But I hurt too badly to move."

Rick gave a weak smile. "At this point, this situation is simply between you, Kara, Geoff, Anna, and God. It needs to stay like this. Your dad and mom—my sweet little sister Rachel—in Sri Lanka certainly do not need to be informed of this. Certainly, don't say anything to your in-laws. Tell Anna not to say anything to her parents. Not to downplay the seriousness of this situation, but this is really a family squabble. Many people would be crushed, bruised, and/or destroyed if they learn about this, even if intimacy was avoided."

"You should know, Uncle Rick," Zach interrupted, "that I told the three of them I was coming to see you this morning and suggested they get someone to take their places at church today. For one thing, I don't know how Geoff could explain his broken nose. I told them I would follow whatever you advised."

"Okay," Richard responded. He then continued, "From what you said, this was not a romantic tryst. It doesn't appear that Kara and Geoff were carrying on an illicit affair of the heart. If we are to believe them—and I know no reason not to—they were trying to help God out. Remember the story of how barren Sarai gave her maid Hagar to Abraham so he could have an heir? Some people are convinced that the present conflict in the Middle East is a continuation of the struggle between Ishmael and Isaac but on a much larger scale. All because Sarah decided to help God. He's almighty God. He doesn't need any help.

"Zach, regardless of how hurt you have been and regardless of what you want to do, you *must* forgive Kara, Geoff, and Anna. If you don't forgive them, you will destroy yourself and your marriage by allowing bitterness to consume your heart. Forgiveness isn't for them; it's for you. You need to pray until God washes away all the hurt and hatred and replaces it with His love.

"As your friend, here's what I want you to do. First, I want you to take a two-month sabbatical from the church and district work. Take Kara and go to the family cabin on Mt. Jefferson. Fall in love again. Renew your commitment to each other and to God. As your superintendent, I'll cover the pulpit for you, so you still will draw your salary from the church. I will speak to the church board. Second, I want you to go home and tell Kara, Geoff, and Anna that you forgive them, that you love them—provided you honestly can say that. Both are decisions you make. Then I want you to be intentional in loving them. Go out of your way to show your love. Get flowers for Kara. Arrange a sitter and send Geoff and Anna away for a weekend vacation. Third, I want you and Kara to go to marriage counselling. There's none better than Dr. William Ellis. I know he is out of state, but you can do the counselling sessions via Zoom. I'll call him and ask that he fit you in right away as a favor to me. And finally, I want you and Kara to go to a fertility specialist. I recommend Dr. Lindvall in Brother Collins's church."

Zach took several deep breaths. Raising his head to look Rick in the eyes, he asked, "Friend Rick, does Uncle Rick and the right reverend agree with you?"

The Reverend Richard S. Tanner's smile reached his eyes. "Uncle Rick is proud of the way you have handled this. Proud that you are reaching out for help. He understands your trauma and shock. He knows you are hurting! Human reaction is to hurt back. Your reaction—though volatile—could have been much worse and devastating to the family and church, both locally and further afield. Uncle Rick is confident the four of you will make it. God is not done with you and Kara yet. His hand is on you for a purpose.

"The right reverend puts familial ties aside." Rick continued. "He is personally concerned for a very dear, young, and successful pastor and his wife and the negative impact this situation could have on all who know them. Your reputation and ministry could be destroyed. Many people who look up to you in your church, in your community, in the district and national levels of our churches, and in your broad circle of friends and acquaintances would be so disappointed that some would never recover and lose confidence in the ministry—even in God.

"The right reverend is not trying to cover up sin. He views this as serious temptation. You did not get drunk. Kara and Geoff did not commit adultery. Being tempted of the devil is not wrong. Yielding to temptation is. With every temptation, Scripture says, He makes a way of escape. The car door slamming into you shin was yours. Your early arrival home was God's way of protecting you, Kara, Geoff, and Anna. You never considered that, did you?

"I repeat, I'm not covering sin. No sinful act was committed. You and the others have repented of any thoughts of sin that you had. But because the right reverend's leadership position in the district, he needs to protect the ministry and shield others from harmful gossip. Was your temptation at the bar any different than Kara and Geoff's in the bedroom? What happened is between you, Kara, Geoff, Anna, and God. That is where it needs to stay. The Bible teaches that if we have anything against our brother—or if he has anything against us— we should *first* go to him *privately* and iron out the differences. *First privately*, not publicly or before witnesses. That's what we are doing in this situation. We're following biblical principles."

"Do you agree?" Rick asked. Zach nodded. "Zach, let's pray before you go," Rick said as he started to kneel by his chair. "You need God's divine love flowing through you. You need His wisdom to lead you. You need the whole armor of God to help you to win the greatest spiritual battle you have ever faced. Come. Kneel with me."

Rick prayed, "Holy Father, You are our only hope in this life. You are the One who provides for us. You are the One who saves us. You are the One who redeems our past mistakes and failures and then molds them into something beautiful that glorifies You.

"Now, Lord, we pray for a special anointing to rest on Zach. You see the turmoil that he has experienced. In Your grace and wisdom, redeem this situation for Your glory. Grant him divine favor and wisdom to allow Your Spirit to lead and guide him as he faces one of the greatest trials of his life. Help him to put on the whole armor of God to equip himself to face his adversary. Clothe him with the helmet of salvation to protect his mind. Let the mind of Christ be formed in him. Clothe him with the breastplate of righteousness to protect his heart. You alone, Lord, are our righteousness. Let truth be belted around his waist. Your Word is truth. Shod his feet with the gospel of peace. Great peace have they that love Thy law, and nothing shall offend them. Above all, give him the shield of faith to deflect the fiery darts of the enemy. Help his hand to firmly grip the sword of the Spirit, which is Your Word. And may every aspect of his life be seasoned with prayer."

They both continued to pray until Zach felt the direction, strength, and peace he needed to face the situation at home.

CHAPTER 5
Sunday, March 5, 2017

Kara, Geoff, and Anna were waiting once again for Zach when he parked in the garage late Sunday evening. The drive home from Uncle Rick's had been peaceful, even relaxing, until he exited the freeway and shortly thereafter turned into the subdivision. As he was pulling into the driveway, he was praying that God would help him to (1) love and forgive Kara, Geoff, and Anna, (2) put the events of the past thirty-six hours in the past, and (3) to regain his faith and confidence in them.

Geoff and Anna were sitting on the sofa and Kara was in the recliner with a throw wrapped around her when he entered the family room. Three pairs of red, stress-filled eyes followed him as he seated himself in the swivel chair near the fireplace. Not knowing how to start, he simply stared at the carpet in the tension-filled room. Finally, he began. Once he began, he couldn't stop.

"Last Friday I came home so excited to surprise Kara and to tell her that I had been elected secretary for the district youth. A birthday surprise! But when I came home and saw Kara and Geoffrey together in the bedroom, I lost it. Big time! Being shocked and dumbfounded were understatements. I couldn't think. I couldn't breathe. I just had to get away. I jumped in the car and just started driving. I didn't care where I went, I just wanted to put distance between me and here. After hours of heading west on the freeway, I stopped for gas and then just meandered country roads. All I could think of was that my marriage was over and so was my ministry. I never felt so broken and helpless. I have never been so angry. I have never been so hate-filled. I have never felt so hopeless. I have never wanted to die before. My world had fallen apart.

"Eventually I came to the intersection of two country highways. There was a bar with flashing neon signs. They beckoned me. The only alcohol I've ever had was once for communion at a church I was visiting. However, I pulled into the parking lot and started to get out of the car. I just wanted to blot out what I had seen and felt.

"As I put my left foot on the ground, a gust of wind slammed the door against my shin. The pain awakened me to my surroundings. Immediately, I felt the hands of God enfolding me, His love surrounding me. I wept. I repented for what I had planned to do; I felt so guilty. I repented for my raging fury and white-hot hatred toward you. I repented for my anger at God.

"But when I got home and saw that you all were still here, I lost it again. I'm sorry for the way I overreacted—both times. I want you to know that I love each of you. I really do. Kara, I love you and want our marriage to not just survive but to thrive. I'm sorry I hit you, Geoff. Anna, I hope you can forgive my insulting words.

"As you know," Zach continued, "I talked to Uncle Rick. I was so confused when I went to talk to him. I told him what I saw and how I reacted. I told him about my fears of my marriage falling apart and my ministry imploding. I told him about the infertility and Anna's solution. I told him about parking in front of the bar. I asked him to talk to me as a friend, not as my favorite uncle or as my mentor and district bishop. I wept like a baby. He simply sat and listened, very stoically, never interrupting me, never showing any emotion. Afterwards, he took my hands and we prayed. Then he asked some very pointed questions. For some, I really struggled with the answers.

"Eventually, he outlined a recovery program for me—for us, Kara. First, I've already confessed my love you. Love is a choice, and I choose to put what happened behind us. I choose to love each of you. I sincerely mean that. I've asked for your forgiveness. Second, Kara and I will take a two-month sabbatical from the church and district. He suggested we go to the family cabin. Third, he recommended marital counseling and gave me the name of an out-of-state counsellor; he said we could do the counselling sessions online via Zoom. Fourth, he wants Kara and me to go to a fertility specialist that's in Brother Collins's church in Greenfield. The counsellor and doctor are men he has worked with over the years; he's confident of their professionalism and discretion.

"I then asked if Uncle Rick and the right reverend agreed with Friend Rick. He had a few extra comments relating to the two separate roles. Uncle Rick's comments were personal, familial, and encouraging. The Right Reverend Tanner's concern was for the negative impact the situation would have on ministry in general and our ministry and reputation in particular if the story were to become known. He stressed the situation is totally between the four of us and God, and it should stay simply between the four of us and God. He doesn't want us to even tell any of our parents.

"One thing Uncle Rick did say is worth repeating. I kind of had lost sight of it. He said being tempted of the devil is not sin; yielding to temptation is. He said Scripture teaches that with every temptation, God makes a way of escape. The door slamming on my shin was mine. My arriving home a day early was yours."

Zach looked at each one to gauge their reactions and asked if they had any questions. Anna was the only one who commented. "I like the four steps that Uncle Rick gave you. I know you reaffirmed for love for us and asked for our forgiveness for your reaction. But, Zachery, I didn't hear that you forgive us. Do you?"

CHAPTER 6
Sunday, March 5, 2017

Zach lowered his eyes to the floor as he answered Anna, "I do. At least I want to." Then he looked at the three of them and quietly said, "That was one of the tough questions Rick asked. I really want to; and I pray that I can. I thought I had when Rick and I prayed just before I left. My problem is that the situation was pre-meditated. It was planned because I was going to be out of town. You premeditatedly planned to break marriage vows and to deceive me."

Anna's penetrating eyes stabbed Zach. "Zach, it was my idea for Kara and Geoff to get together. We did it out of love for you and your desire for children. With you and Geoff being so identical that your own mother has difficulty telling you apart, we knew the DNA would support the claim that you were the father if any tests were ever run. You have danced all around the word *adultery*. We never considered it as such. Under the law of Moses, if a brother died without heirs, his brother was required to marry the widow and raise up children for his brother. To us this was the same situation. To us this was a medical procedure; Geoff would simply be a sperm donor. It wasn't a romantic liaison."

Zach closed his eyes and shook his head. "Anna, you explained this before. You are forgetting something. I am not dead. Geoffrey is already married. We are living in the New Testament and not the Old. The Scripture does not apply. You would have my wife and your husband commit adultery. Adultery by any other name is still adultery. Kara is a pastor's wife; Geoffrey is a missionary kid. And then the three of you were going to lie by your silence and let me tell the world that the child was mine? How long would you be able to cover that lie? Christians don't lie! Remember?"

Zach sighed deeply and looked in the eyes of the three again. "I know nothing happened last Friday because I got home earlier than expected. I refuse to let my mind think about my other out-of-town trips. I want to forgive you all, forget what almost occurred. I really do. I confess I'm not totally there yet. But I'm praying that someday soon I will be."

Zach ran his hand in his pant pocket and felt the gift card. "Oh Geoff, I really do love you and Anna. Take this gift card and take your wife away for a weekend. There's five hundred dollars on the card. I'll cover the babysitting."

"Thanks, Zach," Geoffrey said sarcastically. "I suppose that was Uncle Rick's idea too. Why don't you just keep it until you can forgive us? The three of us acknowledged that we were wrong. We said we all had misgivings, but it seemed like a logical thing to do. We've repented before God and asked you to forgive us. But as Anna, pointed out, you haven't. You have a hard time even looking us in the eye. I suppose your text for Sunday is Matthew 6:12, 'Forgive us our debts, as we also forgive our debtors.'" Turning to take Anna's hand to help her stand, Geoffrey continued, "And just for the record, this was the only time I've been in your bedroom, at least when you haven't been around. It will be my last."

With a sorrowful glance at Kara, Geoff and Anna opened the door to go home. Kara eased herself out of the recliner and stood facing Zach. Her eyes were red; tear tracks marred her face. "What do you want me to do, Zach? Friday you told me to leave. Anna already said I could use their guestroom."

Zach stumbled over his words. "I don't want you to leave me. I thought we would leave for the cabin in a day or two and work on our marriage. If Dr. William Ellis is available, we can begin the marriage counselling at the cabin since it is equipped with Wi-Fi."

Kara raised her eyebrow in response. Quietly she said, "Zach, I only considered getting pregnant by Geoff because I love you. I still do. There's nothing between me and Geoff. He loves Anna. But, Zach, there's no point in me going to the cabin. You're no closer to forgiving me than when you dropped your suitcase and ran out of the house. You said you love me, but your words don't match your eyes. Zach, I've done and said all that I know to do to tell and show you how deeply sorry I am. I always wanted kids, but I'm so glad we don't have any now. At least they will not be affected regardless of what you decide to do about being married to me. If you want, I will say I had an affair so you can divorce me and keep your ministerial license." A sob escaped as Kara turned toward the hallway and said, "I'm going to sleep in the guestroom."

Zach sank to the carpet, buried his face in his hands as his arms encircled his knees, and wept.

CHAPTER 7
Monday, March 6, 2017

Zach was asleep, still slumped on the family room carpet, when Kara stepped into the kitchen the next morning. She reached for the coffee pot, forgetting she failed to set it last night. She sat the coffee mug on the counter, grabbed her purse, and walked into the garage. She had a few errands to run and decided to start at Starbucks.

An hour later with two places ticked off her list, Kara picked up her phone and then quickly replaced it in her purse when she saw Zach was calling. She didn't feel like talking to him today. She still had a few places to go. He could go to the cabin if he wanted; it would be good for him to learn how to pack for himself for a change.

Three and a half hours later, Kara was disappointed that Zach's car was still in the garage. She decided to make a sandwich and then take a nap in the guestroom. She wasn't sleepy but she wanted to avoid seeing or talking to Zach.

However, Zach was sitting at the kitchen bar, sipping coffee, waiting for Kara. He was still in his clothes from yesterday, his eyes red from crying. He reached to hug Kara, but she pulled away and moved to the refrigerator. "Kara, wait. Can we talk? I spent most of the night praying. God showed me I've been wrong. I forgive you and Geoff and Anna. Please forgive me."

Kara turned toward Zach, her face devoid of any emotion. She stared at him and waited for him to say something. He opened his mouth and then closed it. She started to walk away, and he said, "Kara, wait. I'm sorry. I know I was wrong too. Please forgive me. Let's erase the last four days and start over again. Please!"

"I would like nothing more," Kara replied, "if you really have forgiven me."

"I have. As I said, I prayed most of the night, just sitting on the floor. The Lord showed me I'm at fault for not forgiving you and Geoff and Anna. I'm sorry! I love you! I want us to be whole again. Let's work together." Zach walked over and placed his arms around Kara's neck. "Come away with me to the cabin. We'll forget Friday, Saturday, Sunday, and today ever happened."

CHAPTER 8
Sunday, May 14, 2017

The sabbatical was the first real vacation Zach and Kara had taken in five years. The work of the church demanded so much time. They were lucky if they had two free nights a week. Most evenings, Zach met with one or more groups of volunteers, taught home Bible studies, conducted visitation and counselling sessions, or prepared sermons. It felt so good to be at the cabin to simply relax, to curl up with a book on the deck, or even to listen to the birds chirping, and hopefully reconnect and start to heal.

The cabin was really a misnomer. Zach's great grandfather Timothy Tanner had built the cabin as a getaway. The original cabin was a 10' by 16' living/dining/kitchen with two sets of bunk beds. Toilet facilities were outside along the path leading to the lake. Zack's grandfather William Tanner added in-door plumbing, a master bedroom suite, and three bedrooms for his three kids, Richard (Rick), Zach's mother Rachel, and the youngest, Rebekkah, whose husband Emmanuel Montez now pastored in Texas. Richard and his brothers-in-law had enlarged the great room to include a modern kitchen and updated bathrooms. They also took advantage of the steep sloping terrain to create a lower level with additional bedrooms, two bathrooms, and a game room with a large deck on top. It was an ideal location for the family to meet to celebrate holidays and special occasions. Even with several family members involved in global ministries, the cabin served as a homing beacon. As the patriarch of the family, Richard kept track of the use of the cabin and its upkeep.

The two months sped by. They had stocked the cupboards and freezer when they first arrived. Their days were free except for the time they set aside at the beginning of the day for devotions and their weekly marriage counselling sessions on Thursday afternoons. Everything else was done spontaneously. They slept late and ate when they wanted to. Then they decided whether to fish, hike, nap, read, put a jigsaw puzzle together, or explore the quaint towns around the lake. They had no plans but to get reacquainted, renew their love for each other, and become spiritually rejuvenated.

With the car packed to return home, Zach and Kara took one more hike along the lake. Kara broke the comfortable silence saying, "Zach, I really enjoyed the time here. It's been fun! Let's make time to come here at least once a quarter. And when you go out of town to conferences or to preach, I want to go with you. I think spending time with you is more important than directing the daycare. My assistant can cover for me when I'm gone. She's very capable."

Zach pulled her close and kissed her. "I like those ideas. With your other responsibilities at home and at the church, I don't see how you have time to direct the daycare anyway. Maybe you should think about promoting your assistant."

The church welcomed them back as the dearly beloved couple they were. Their faces glowed as they accepted the greetings and love. Without going into detail, Zach express their pleasure in being back at the church and publicly thanked Bishop Richard Tanner for filling the pulpit in his absence.

After the Sunday service, it was evident that some wanted details why the sabbatical was necessary. Zach and Kara just said how wonderful it was to be back.

CHAPTER 9
Tuesday, October 17, 2017

Four months passed before they could get an appointment with Dr. Lindvall at the fertility center. Zach signed a waiver so the doctor could access his medical records concerning the motorcycle accident. Doctor Lindvall also did a battery of tests on both Zach and Kara. They were nervous as they waited to talk to the doctor in mid-October.

"It's nice to see you again, Pastor and Mrs. Petersen. Is it okay if I call you Zach and Kara?" Dr. Lindvall asked, not really waiting for an answer. "I think I have good news for you."

"Zach, I understand why your doctor thought you might have difficulty becoming a father. The impact of the motorcycle's frame crashing into your groin crushed your pubic bone and caused numerous fractures to your pelvis. The jagged metal almost caused castration. However, your bones have healed, and you had a top-flight urological surgeon. Your plumbing works fine. Test results show minor scar tissue. Your sperm count is low but still within the normal range. The infertility problems you and Kara have had over the last seven years do not seem to be caused by the accident. I know you have blamed yourself, but I cannot determine any reason why you cannot become a father.

"Kara," Dr. Lindvall continued, "am I correct in assuming this is your first gynecology appointment since your premarital exam? The OB/GYN you listed is out of state, and you don't seem to have one locally. The test results indicate a few factors causing you to have difficulty conceiving. First, your uterus has a slight deformity. Second, your cycle is irregular. Third, you have some endometriosis which may be partially blocking the fallopian tubes. Separately these things are not a big deal; together they can decrease the ability to conceive. The good news is that two of these problems can be corrected with minimally invasive surgery. And I can prescribe medication to regulate your cycles."

Zach smiled at this news while Kara covered her mouth and turned pale as tears filled her eyes. She grabbed her purse and hurried from the office. Rising to go after Kara, "Doctor," Zach began, "I don't know why she's reacting this way. I think it's good news. We will be in contact with you to schedule the surgeries. Please send the prescription to Walgreens. You should have the number on file."

Zach found Kara crying softly in their car. "What's wrong, sweetheart? This is all good news!"

Kara turned and looked at him with the color drained from her face. "It is good news, Zach. But don't you see? If I had slept with Geoff, nothing would have happened! I'm the problem, not you. I would not have gotten pregnant. I would have just broken my marriage vows. I can't believe I let Anna convince me it was the right thing to do! Oh, Zach! I'm so sorry, Zach! We didn't do anything, but we almost did. I'm so sorry," she wailed, hiding her face in her hands.

Wrapping Kara in his arms, Zach gently said, "But nothing happened, Kara. God timed my coming home at the right time. I've forgiven you, Geoff, and Anna. You forgave me for overreacting. Let's go home and make another appointment to discuss the surgery or surgeries with Dr. Lindvall. He's sending the prescription to Walgreens."

Six weeks later, in early December, Kara was recovering from minor surgery. It would have been considered outpatient surgery if her blood pressure hadn't dropped and the doctor kept her overnight in the hospital for observation.

Five months later, in May 2018, the home pregnancy test showed positive. Zach took Kara to Sam Wilson's Meat Market, her favorite restaurant, to celebrate although they decided to wait for official confirmation before telling anyone else. The baby should be born in February 2019.

CHAPTER 10
Thursday, May 19, 2021

Zach was beside himself.

Kara's first pregnancy was textbook perfect. She suffered little morning sickness. Baby Sara met or surpassed all markers for a normal, healthy baby. It seemed like Sara had read Dr. Lindvall's manual. The labor was short. The delivery easy. Now Sara was a two-and-a-half-year-old toddler and was into everything, just like the textbooks said she would be.

This pregnancy was Kara's fourth. Number two and three resulted in miscarriages. Every horrible thing Zach had heard from other men seemed to be true on this go around. Her morning sickness lasted well beyond the first trimester and was much more severe than in the first pregnancy. Fear of miscarrying plagued her. She had trouble sleeping. She gained too much weight. She had huge hormonal swings. Zach couldn't do anything right.

The doctor placed her on complete bedrest for the last month before Sophie was born. Now she was experiencing postpartum depression. Some days she couldn't leave the bed. And Zach still could not do anything to please her. Whatever he did was wrong. And, of course, Sara's being a normal two-year-old only added to Zach's anxiety and frustration.

Zach didn't know what to do. He prayed and fasted, asking God to restore his loving wife. He offered to fly Kara's mother out to help her. That resulted in another row. Kara interpreted the offer as a sign Zach thought she was failing as a mother and wife. However, his work at the church was suffering. Consequently, he hired a part-time housekeeper/babysitter to relieve some of the stress on both him and Kara.

Three weeks later, Zach noticed a change. Kara was acting more like her old self and taking more interest in her appearance, Sara and Sophie, and her house. He finally ventured to ask her about the change.

She smiled and said, "I was listening to praise music two weeks or so ago. One line from an old Bill Gaither song said, 'I'll praise Him with the joy that comes from knowing I have held back nothing. And He is Lord!' Then Casting Crowns sang, 'Every tear I've cried, You hold in your hand. You never left my side. And though my heart is torn, I will praise you in this storm.'

"I realized I had allowed the troubles from the pregnancy to throw me into depression. It was devastating; I couldn't do anything. Consequently, I had lost my praise. And yeah, I know you and Dr. Lindvall mentioned post-partum depression, but I blamed feeling down on my lack of sleep, the baby's constant crying with cholic, and being overweight. So, as I listened to those songs and others, I realized I had to renew my praise. I was blaming the kids for me feeling bad when I should have been thanking God for allowing us to have them after almost eight years of barrenness.

"I decided to praise God and to no longer be depressed. Praising God really is a decision, you know. Regardless of our circumstances, He's worthy of honor and praise. It's been a struggle, but I'm doing better. I'm conscientiously trying to praise God and offer thanks for even the insignificant things in life. I'm so sorry for the chaos I put you through. Please forgive me. If you still would like to fly Mom out to help for a few weeks, I would appreciate it.

"I've also been thinking about what Dr. Lindvall said about the dangers of another pregnancy," Kara continued. "I would like a son. However, if you agree, Zach, I think Sophie completes our family. I really got scared a few times during this last pregnancy and would prefer not to go through that trauma again. And I'm sure you do not want to experience the extreme mood changes again."

Zach agreed.

CHAPTER 11
Friday, March 6, 2026

Zach, Kara, Sara, and Sophie were on their way home from the ministers' conference. The ministerial body had elected Zach as the global missions director for the state. Life was good. He had a loving wife, two beautiful kids, a lovely home, a growing church, and a great church staff. He felt contented and smiled as he pulled into the driveway of their home.

Zach parked and woke Sara and Sophie up. He freed Sophie from the car seat's restraints, stood her on the payment, and told her to rush into the house while he grabbed the suitcases from the trunk. He handed Sophie her blue ball before gently swatting her on her training pants to send her off.

Zach's head was deep in the trunk when he heard the squeal of brakes and smelled burning rubber. He immediately turned and saw a car stopped feet past the driveway. The stunned and distraught driver opened the car door and cried, "I didn't see her! Oh God! I'm sorry! I didn't see her!"

The words made no sense until Zach looked behind the car and saw Sophie laying on the ground in a puddle of blood. Zach froze in his tracks and vomited. Attracted by the noise, Kara ran to her baby in the road.

Thankfully, the sixty-something driver in a burgundy jogging suit and matching hair had the presence to call 911. The ever-increasing blare of the siren announced the coming of the ambulance. As if unable to comprehend what had happened, Zach stared at the still body on the ground. Then he noticed the blue ball across the street. With a gasp, he slumped to the ground in a faint.

The paramedics quickly accessed Sophie's injuries and gently placed her on the stretcher. By this time, elderly Mr. Clark, a neighbor, had revived Zach, who still seemed incoherent. Mrs. Clark picked up a crying Sara and took her to her home. Kara rushed over to Zach and said she was riding in the ambulance to Children's Hospital. Mr. Clark volunteered to drive Zach there.

The police came and took a statement from the driver. Since it obviously was a horrible accident, they would not bring any charges against the traumatized lady. Her quick reflexes caused her to jerk the car to the left, thereby hitting Sophie with a glancing blow from the right front fender instead of straight on, which would probably have been fatal.

Kara called Geoff and asked him to meet them at the hospital. Then she called her mother and asked her to fly out to be with them and to watch Sara.

Zach and Mr. Clark arrived at the hospital while the triage nurse was still evaluating Sophie's injuries. She had a broken arm and collarbone, deep gashes in her scalp from hitting rocks on the payment, swelling of the brain, and possible internal injuries besides the road rash. Geoff arrived shortly thereafter. He suggested Mr. Clark go home, and he would make sure Zach and Kara got home.

Eventually, Dr. Marler came to speak to Kara and Zach. "You are lucky your child is alive. Her puffy coat helped to protect her from more serious injuries. You know about the broken bones, the lacerations in the scalp, the swelling of the brain, and probable concussion. Her spleen is damaged, and the surgeon may have to remove it. The next twelve hours will show if she has any other internal injuries. I'm cautiously optimistic, but she's in critical condition. She's going to the PICU. You can go see her there in about twenty minutes. Do you have any questions?"

Zach hung his head as his shoulders slumped. He turned his back and started walking down the hall to the entrance. Geoff ran after him and grabbed his arm. "Hey, Zach, you can't run away. I know you don't like to face things like this, but Sophie and Kara need you now. You owe it to them to step up and be the rock and shelter they need."

Tears filled Zach's eyes. "You don't understand. I caused this. I gave her the ball and told her to go inside. The ball must have slipped from her hands, and she went running after it. The ball was on the other side of the street. It's my fault if my daughter doesn't live!"

"Zach, it's not your fault. It was an accident. No one blames you. But you're needed now." Geoff pulled on Zach's arm and said, "Let's get Kara and go up to the PICU waiting room."

Kara wrapped her arms around Zach's neck and buried her face on his chest. "I went through hell for this baby, and I'm not going to let the devil take her from us!"

"I'm sorry, Kara. Don't blame the devil. It's my fault! I gave Sophie her ball and told her to run inside. The ball apparently slipped out of her hands, and she then ran into the street to get it. I was busy unloading the car when I should have been paying attention to her. I'm sorry!" Zach cried remorsefully.

Kara shook her head and tightly hugged Zach.

Sophie looked so fragile with the multiple tubes and wires connected to her battered body. Bandages encircled her head to protect the stitched gashes. She was heavily sedated and lay motionless. A soft cast, supported by a neck sling, covered her arm. Zach, Kara, and Geoff gathered around the bed and prayed. And then waited.

Early the following morning, a surgeon removed half of Sophie's spleen. The swelling in the brain was less. The nurses were reducing the level of sedation, hoping for a response from Sophie. After Zach, Kara, and Geoff gathered around the bed and thanked God that Sophie seemed to be improving, Geoff drove Zach home to pick up his SUV and check on Sara. In the late afternoon, he would meet his mother-in-law at the airport. He was so thankful that she was able to get a flight so quickly.

When Zach and his mother-in-law stopped by the hospital on their way home, Sophie was alert and thrilled to see her GiGi. The nurses had moved her to regular room. They also had removed some of the tubes and wires as her brain had almost returned to normal size. They had also replaced the swath of gauze around her head with smaller bandages. Zach felt optimistic and offered silent praise to God for protecting his baby from more severe injuries and gave thanks for the vast improvement.

Six days later, Sophie was happy to be home. It would take several more weeks for the bones to heal and for her to fully recover.

Zach knew he needed to talk to Kara about freezing up at the accident, but he didn't know how to approach it. Finally, he pulled her aside and simply said, "Kara, I'm sorry I freaked out when I saw Sophie lying in the street. Seeing her in the blood made me literally sick. Then when I saw the ball across the street, I knew the accident was my fault. My world went black. Kara, I'm so sorry for failing you and Sophie."

Kara smiled and said, "It's alright. She's going to be fine. No one blames you for the accident. No one. You need to forgive yourself. Let's just praise God that Sophie is home!"

CHAPTER 12
Monday, June 4, 2029

Three years later, Zach and Kara and the two growing girls bubbled over with excitement as they boarded the flight in Atlanta enroute to Sri Lanka. Zack and Kara would both be ministering in the national conference later in the week on Thursday, Friday, and Saturday morning. While Zack and Geoff had spent their first eighteen years in Sri Lanka, this would be the first time Kara, Sara, and Sophie had visited there. The kids were excited to see their grandparents and to see where their father and uncle had grown up.

The focus, of course, was the national convention, but Grandma and Grandpa had also planned an itinerary centered around the girls. They would spend the first night in Galle on the southern coast at a hotel noted for its infinity swimming pool that seemed to stretch to the horizon. Although this area had been severely damaged by the tsunami in 2004, new hotels and pristine beaches made this a prime tourist destination. They would also visit the Buddhist Golden Temple at Dumbulla, the royal palace at Kandy, and a tea plantation operated by a childhood friend of Zach and Geoff. Then they would end up at the Pinnawala Elephant Orphanage. There the girls—and adults— could wash elephants as they bathed at the river. And they did.

CHAPTER 13
Thursday, August 9, 2035
Six years later

Ever since the incident years ago, Zach and Kara always traveled together to conferences and speaking engagements. Both were popular speakers and in great demand. Unfortunately, a scheduling conflict arose that was unavoidable. Dr. Kara Petersen, who had earned her Ph.D. in early childhood education, was one of speakers at the national Christian Education/Children's Ministries conference in St. Louis.

Staff members had mailed promotional materials months earlier. Kara's mother was coming to stay with the kids. Zach had already bought their non-refundable tickets when it became evident that he would have to stay behind. They were wanting to expand the church sanctuary, and the architect's only available appointment for the next several months was during the middle of the conference. Geoff was also going with Anna and Kara to golf with his buddies while the women attended meetings.

However, in the morning before the schedule appointment with the architect, Zach received a call for the architect's personal assistant stating the architect's teenage son had been in an auto accident. They would have to postpone the meeting. They scheduled a new date four months out. Since they cancelled the appointment and since he already had a ticket, Zach decided to join the group at the conference. He too would take his golf clubs.

It was going on 8:00 in the evening when Zach arrived at the hotel. He knew it was too late to shower and dress for the evening service. Instead, he ordered room service, kicked back in the recliner, and drifted into a deep sleep.

Noise in the hallway awakened Zach. Groggily he waited as the laughter got louder, and he heard the door open. "Let's get you in bed," he heard his brother say as he saw him loosen his tie. That was when Kara noticed Zach in the recliner. The three remained speechless.

Finally, Zach said tightly, "The last time I saw this situation, I overreacted and broke your nose, Geoff. Would you care to explain why you want *my* wife in bed? Or perhaps, my wife would like to explain why she brought my twin brother back to her hotel room? Am I interrupting something I should know about?"

Kara sat on the bed and closed her eyes. A few moments later she said, "Zach, I've been having some neurological problems for the past few months. Dizziness. Fatigue. Poor muscle coordination. Weakness. Double vision. Dr. Gray has been doing some tests, but nothing is conclusive yet. He's thinking in terms of lupus, MS, or perhaps a tumor. I didn't tell you because I knew you would not handle it well. You never do. The only ones who know are Anna and Geoff. I was going to tell you after this conference. Dr. Gray recommended that I cancel all future speaking engagements until he can figure out what's going on and prescribe a treatment.

"I asked Geoff to stand by tonight because I was dizzy. If I had problems speaking tonight, I wanted him nearby to help me off the stage. When these problems occur, the only thing that really seems to help is taking some sample medicine Dr. Gray gave me and sleeping. That's why Geoff recommended I hop in bed."

"And taking my tie off is just something I do as soon as I can. Regardless of what you are thinking, brother," Geoff interrupted, "I have no designs on your wife! I was only trying to be a good brother-in-law and make sure she got to her room safely. Anna rode up in the elevator with us but got off earlier because we are two floors down and have our two teens with us." Geoff glared at Zach and continued, "You really have a problem trusting those who love you the most, bro."

Zach stared at the carpet with his hands fisted on his knees. "Well, say something!" Geoff barked.

Tears filled Zach's eyes as he said, "I can't process this. It's like a video of the *incident* is looped, repeating, and repeating. I keep seeing you jerking your hands from her shoulder and waist. The range of emotions I saw in that second was unbelievable. Shock. Fear. Embarrassment. Guilt. Remorse. Pity." He looked up at Kara and Geoff. "I do trust you! It was just so shocking to see both come in together. Geoff is jerking his tie off and saying, 'Let's get you in bed.' The flashback was terrifying.

"And then to realize, Kara, that you were afraid to tell me about your health. Have I really failed you that much? We all know I have always had a weak stomach. I don't do blood and guts. Remember when I almost passed out when Dr. Berwald said I would have to help you clean the wound when he removed that lump from your hand? But I love you. I'm sorry I'm not what you need," Zach concluded, tears flowing freely down his cheeks.

"Go on to bed, Kara. I'm going for a walk." Zach excused himself, leaving Kara and Geoff looking at each other.

The room was still dark when Kara woke up the next morning. She reached over to awaken Zach, only to find his side of the bed still made. He had not slept in it last night. She checked the suite's recliner and sofa but did not find Zach. She checked the bathroom; he was not there.

She picked up her phone. "Geoff, Zach didn't come back last night. I don't know what to do."

"Kara," Geoff replied, "Zach's a big boy; he can take care of himself. Your potential diagnosis is a lot to swallow. It's always taken Zach time to process things like this. He's never been one to be spontaneous. He has always had to analyze the pros and cons of any decision or new situation. I'm sure he's trying to figure out how the family will adapt to the reality that Momma's not going to be able to continue to do everything she has been. I know he loves you. I know when he said for better or for worse, he really meant that. He will be there for you and Sara and Sophie. Just give him time to process everything. Meet Anna and me downstairs for breakfast in an hour."

Zach was inserting his keycard in the lock when Kara opened the door to go downstairs, causing him to stumble. She grabbed his arm to keep him from falling and then waited for him to say something. "That was a lot to assimilate last night. I walked for a couple of hours last night and then fell asleep on a park bench," he explained. "I'm going to shower and then I'll meet you downstairs for breakfast."

CHAPTER 14
Sunday, September 19, 2036
One year later

No one said anything about Kara and Geoff's encounter with Zach during the conference or even after. They all pretended nothing had happened. The only evidence of any changes was Kara cutting back her responsibilities at the church, cancelling her three pending speaking engagements—one international—and having more appointments with Dr. Gray. Zach wanted to go with her to the doctor appointments, but she found an excuse to discourage him every time. However, he noticed subtle changes to her stamina and cognitive acuity. He felt excluded and resented her privacy.

As the leaves began changing colors, Kara said nervously, "Zach, I have an appointment tomorrow with Dr. Gray. Would you like to come with me?"

"Tomorrow? I can't. I have to get ready for the quarterly meeting tomorrow night with the trustees. If you had let me know about your appointment last week, I could have worked my schedule around to be free. Sorry."

"Can you change it?" she asked timidly.

"Can you change your appointment with the doctor? The date for this trustee meeting was set last fall when we established the church calendar for the new year."

"Zach, I would really like for you to come with me."

"Really? I wanted to go with you to your earlier appointments, but you shot me down till I finally gave up asking. You've excluded me all these months. The only insight I have is an occasional cryptic remark from Geoff. I'm not good enough to tell what's going on with you, but you can tell Anna and Geoff. That's an idea! Call Geoff. Maybe he can go with you."

Zach saw Kara flinch as he flung the last barb. Zach knew he had hit home. Petty? Yes. Did it make him feel better? Not necessarily. He wanted to drop everything and hear what Dr. Gray had to say. However, he could not postpone preparing for the meeting. Maybe this was the wake-up call that Kara needed. How could she continue to exclude him and still expect him to support her? These last several months certainly had qualified as "for worse." What was that cliché about ships passing in the night? Would she even miss him if he slept in the guest room? He was glad Sara was living in the dorms this term.

The Monday night trustee meeting was over by 8:30. They rubber stamped three proposals that Zach submitted and hired a new worship pastor. Zach smiled at that. When he was a kid in Sri Lanka, they had "song leaders" who were volunteers, not paid staff members. But then, the music was not as polished.

Kara was sitting in the recliner with a Diet Coke when Zach passed through the family room from the garage. Kara looked up, and he saw the tears and red eyes. "What's wrong, sweetheart?" Zach asked, kneeling beside her.

"Dr. Gray said the last MRI showed a small tumor in the frontal lobe of my brain. It's putting pressure on the optical nerve, which is causing the problems with my vision and dizziness. He wants to consult with a couple of neurosurgeons to see if they recommend removing it. He's not sure what is causing some of the other problems like the muscle weakness, the pain, and overall fatigue."

"So, what is he recommending now?" Zach asked.

"Now we wait...Zach, I'm so scared; I've tried to be strong and not bother you!" she sobbed.

Zach enfolded her in his arms. "What do you want me to do?"

"Hold me."

Zach picked her up and then placed her on his lap as he took his place in the recliner. He squeezed her and gently prayed till her sobs subsided. He berated himself for not going with her. But maybe this would convince her that she still needed him.

CHAPTER 15
Thursday, October 29, 2036

Zach drove Kara to her next appointment with Dr. Gray. The doctor welcomed them and asked them to take a seat in his spacious office. "Kara, I shared your medical records with Dr. Liu and her colleague Dr. Frank. We're fairly sure the tumor is benign but can't be sure without a biopsy. Of course, a biopsy of a brain tumor is invasive. Instead, Doctors Liu and Frank are recommending stereotactic radiosurgery.

"Stereotactic radiosurgery is probably a new term to you. It is a non-invasive method to treat small, benign spine and brain tumors. It uses high energy radiation to destroy tumors or other abnormalities," Dr. Gray explained. "By small, I mean less than 3 cm. Your is 2.5 cm.

"Stereotactic radiosurgery is bloodless. It does not require an incision to the skull. Instead, it uses specialized computer-assisted equipment for targeted treatment. The patient receives one to five treatments and can normally return home shortly after the last one. What do you think?" Dr. Gray asked.

"I'm totally overwhelmed, totally relieved," Kara replied. "I was expecting chemotherapy and/or radiation and then traditional surgery. I was thinking that I would reject the chemo. Sometimes the side effects of the chemo seem worse than the disease. And frankly, I didn't want to lose my hair. I haven't cut it since I was six years old and played Mulan."

"Mulan, huh? I would have thought you more of a Jasmine instead of Mulan," the doctor smiled. "Back to the stereotactic radiosurgery. If you agree, I will have Donna set an appointment with Dr. Liu. As you are aware, she practices at Henry Ford Hospital in Detroit. It has the latest equipment in the Upper Midwest. A nearby apartment tower provides lodging for patients' families and interns. Donna can make arrangement for your stay there when she set your appointment with Dr. Liu. Do you have any questions?"

"Yes," Zach answered. "What is the success rate of this procedure? How does it differ from the Gamma knife that did nothing to help my cousin? What are the odds of the tumor reoccurring?"

"Good questions," Dr. Gray began as he leaned back in his chair and turned toward his credenza. Gathering several pamphlets and giving them to Zach, he said, "I think these will answer your questions. If not, give me a call and we can set up a consultation before you go to Detroit."

CHAPTER 16
Tuesday, January 5, 2038

The stereotactic radiosurgery was successful. It destroyed the tumor and released the pressure on the optic nerve. Kara's sight was improving. Dr. Gray still wanted to do further testing to determine the cause of Kara's pain, shortness of breath, and overall fatigue.

Consequently, five weeks after the radiosurgery, Kara was back in the hospital. Lying in her hospital bed, she squeezed Zach's hand. "I'm so tired of being tired and tired of tests. I'll be glad when this is all over."

"I know, honey," Zach replied. "We've spent more nights at the hospital in the last few years than we have in hotel rooms, although we had plenty of those too. If I understand Dr. Gray correctly, he thinks a lot of your problems stem from an autoimmune disease, but so far, he has been unable to identify it. At least the scary stuff should be behind us. I was more worried about yeast infection on your heart valve than the brain tumor. The infectious disease doctor and the cardiologist both had to work together to treat the yeast infection. I didn't know if you were going to survive the ampho–, whatever that medicine was."

"Amphotericin," Kara supplied. "I didn't know if I would either. Zach, I will not take that again. Heaven is too close for me to endure those 'shake and bake' treatments again. The chills. The fever. The nausea. The headaches. I love you and want to spend many more years with you, but I will not take that again. Don't even ask if Dr. Koldin should ever suggest it again!"

Five days later, Dr. Gray stopped by Kara's private room. "Good. I'm glad you're here, Zach. I want to go over the tests results with Kara." Turning to Kara and smiling, he said, "You are complicated case, young lady. As I explained before, you have symptoms of lupus and MS, but we can't find the markers for a definitive diagnosis for either one. Either way, by treating the symptoms, the medicines you are on seem to be helping. We'll label the constant pain as fibromyalgia, but I think some unknown, underlying factors are involved. Your leaky heart valve causes some of the chronic fatigue. However, your cardiologist doesn't want to replace it yet. The abdominal pain we will label as irritable bowel syndrome.

"I'm going to release you to go home tomorrow. But I want to get another chest x-ray this afternoon to compare with the ones earlier in the year. This will help us monitor the scarring in your lungs."

Turning to Zach, Dr. Gray said, "Take care of her, Zach. She's a trooper. With everything she has been through over the years, I have never heard her complain. She's yelped a few times when I pushed on this or that. But I've never heard her whine or pity herself. She's a remarkable lady!"

CHAPTER 17
Tuesday, April 23, 2041

Three years later, Zach looked down at a panting Kara, who was sitting on a stone outcropping overlooking Athens, Greece. "Kara, I'm sorry. I shouldn't have brought you on this trip. I didn't realize there would be so much walking or so many stairs," Zach apologized.

"Hey, after the stress of Moriah's wedding last month, I needed a break. Just give me a few minutes to rest and we can go again," Kara panted. "You told me I should probably stay home. But when else would I get to see the Parthenon, walk in the ruins of Philippi, or visit the **monasteries** at Meteora?

"Because of your fear of heights, I know you didn't look down from the towering rock pillars the monasteries sit on, but they were so cool! They're like fingers soaring up from the basin. It's amazing the priests were able to build such beautiful churches on the top of such shear rocks. You know the monks had to hoist all the building material up by rope and pulley. Amazing!

"Just give me a few minutes to catch my breath. If I can climb to the top of the Mayan temple in Belize, I can make it to top of the Acropolis. I'm not going to be this close to the Parthenon and not be able to touch the pillars."

"Yes, ma'am," Zach sighed. "But remember it's been a few years and a few surgeries since you scaled the temple in Belize. You're not as strong as you were."

"You keep singing that same old song. When are you going to quit? Here, help me up. Let's go," Kara commanded.

46

CHAPTER 18
Friday, July 17, 2048
Seven years later

Kara loved Ukraine. This was her third trip to the breadbasket of Europe since the Russian invasion in 2022. She had curtailed most of her international travel, but the chance to be in Ukraine again was impossible to pass up. She was one of the featured speakers at the children's ministry conference in Kyiv. Sunday afternoon, she and Zach would fly home after he ministered in the morning service. Then they were going to spend three weeks at the family cabin. However, first she had to get through the children's rally tonight and the two workshops Saturday morning. Zach had insisted that he take her back to the hotel to rest this afternoon.

Reluctantly, Kara had to admit that Zach was right. Traveling—especially internationally—and speaking at conferences were getting too taxing on her health. This probably would be her last overseas trip. Nevertheless, she was excited about the evening service.

Her topic tonight was one very dear to her heart because it was so personal. She knew from personal experience what she would be preaching about. Her title was "The Second Dedication."

It is always a joyous occasion when young parents dedicate their babies or young children to the Lord, pledging to train the child to love the Lord, to walk in His precepts, and to follow His will. This is the first dedication. It's much like Hannah dedicating young Samuel to divine service. In reality, it's a dedication of the parents to set the example before the child.

The second dedication usually come eighteen to twenty-eight years later. This is when parents reap what they have sown in their children. Since infancy they taught their children to seek first the kingdom of God, to put God first in all aspects of life, and to follow Him, regardless of where He leads or what the cost. But what if that involves an eighteen-year-old daughter, such as Sophie, wanting to go of a short-term mission trip to Kenya? What if the will of God calls a young married couple to leave the confines of North America to minister in third-world countries in Asia, Africa, or Central America? What if that means the parents will not be able to watch their grandchildren grow up? That's when the parents have to dedicate their children to the will of God once again. Hence, the second dedication. Instead of a dedication of training, the second is a dedication of releasing their children to follow the will of God.

Early on, the parents realize that dedicating their children to the Lord is really an act of consecrating themselves to the will of God. The dedication does not save the child or give it membership in the church. That will be the child's decision later in life. The first dedication promises the parents will instill in their children the desire to live a life consecrated to Christ. That's pretty easy when it's a matter of nightly devotions with the children and making sure they're on time for Sunday school and regular services. It gets a bit more difficult to taxi the children to youth services and be counsellors for youth camps. Then later it's guiding the children as they look toward college and decide on a career.

The second dedication comes when parental control is lessening and the parents watch to see how effective their parenting has been. The second dedication is an affirmation that the parents still want their children to walk in the ways of the Lord, regardless of where that will may lead. And regardless the sacrifice the parents must make to facilitate that.

Kara often thought about the forty-five years Zach and Geoff's parents served in Sri Lanka. They went as a young married couple and raised their children at the mission's compound in Colombo.

Consequently, Zach's grandparents and aunts and uncles only saw the boys ever four to five years when the family furloughed. Now Kara was facing the same thing as Sophie and her husband, Dr. Steve Black, would be joining the staff at the Bible college in Zambia and, of course, taking their children with them.

CHAPTER 19
Wednesday, July 24, 2058
Ten years later

It had been ten years since Zach and Kara made their last trip to Ukraine. Time flew by so quickly. He couldn't help but smile as he took the bouquet of balloons and flowers from the delivery man and walked through the front door. Today was Kara's birthday. She was sixty-eight years old. She and Zach were both born in 1990. The flowers were just a ploy to throw Kara off track.

Zach had tried desperately over the past two months to keep the surprise party a secret from Kara. The ladies' ministry at their church insisted on celebrating with a lavish party tonight in the fellowship hall. This being the regular Bible study night, Kara would think nothing of dressing and going to church. He hoped she would wear her long, grey hair in her typical but classy chignon. That was Zach's preferred hair style for is wife. Could Zach suggest she wear something more "Sunday morning" dressy instead of "Wednesday night" casual without tipping her off? Maybe he could if he got her a corsage to wear. The plan was to have the regular worship service just like a regular Bible study, but then Zach would direct everyone to go to the fellowship hall.

Zach was concerned about Kara's health. She continued to lose weight. Although she never complained, she was rarely pain free, even with the pain medication. The cardiologist continued to monitor her heart. The pulmonologist checked her lungs every six months. The rattles and scratches in her lungs from the scarring from her many bouts of bronchitis had stayed basically the same for the past few years. Her last MRI showed that the brain tumor had not reoccurred. However, he could tell she wasn't quite as sharp as she once was. Her humorous quips were not as quick.

The fellowship hall was beautifully decorated. Two rows of chairs lined three sides of the room. Tulle and tiny white lights covered the walls. Four tables containing plates, cutlery, and a wide assortment of finger foods formed spokes from the hub of a circular table ladened with a large, three-layer birthday cake. In the southwest corner, a videographer was filming couples posing with a life-size cutout of Kara as they commented on Kara's life. The northwest corner held a decorated pergola with two recliners for the guest of honor and her husband of forty-seven years. Drink and dessert stations were set around the room.

The ladies did all the planning, so Zach was surprised by the program. It included several speakers intimately acquainted with Kara's life, such as her childhood best friend, her college roommate, her maid of honor, and two members from the local congregation, and a narrated video of snapshots from Kara's life. The narrator's voice sounded familiar although purposely disguised. As the video neared its conclusion, the narrator's voice changed as Sophie, mic in hand, and her three children stepped from behind the large screen, concluding the presentation by wishing her mother an incredibly happy birthday.

Kara smiled brightly as she stood to respond to the accolades and the surprised family members who had flown in from Africa. Her steps faltered as she gasped, clutched her heart, and passed out.

CHAPTER 20
Thursday, July 25, 2058

Zach, Sophie, and Sara sat in the ICU waiting room. Geoff, Anna, and several members of the church waited with them. A team of doctors had been constantly working with Kara and evaluating her condition. She had never awakened from the first heart attack and had a second attack in the ambulance enroute to the hospital.

His face drawn, Dr. Dawson walked over to Zach. "May I speak to you in the consultation room?" he asked.

Zach forced a smile and said, "All of these here are family and/or members of our church. You can tell all of us, but I think I know what you are going to say."

"Pastor Petersen," Dr. Dawson began, "there is no way to make this easy. Medically the team has done everything we can for your wife. She is unresponsive. Her lungs are filling with fluid. Her kidney function is dropping. It's only a matter of time. She might have survived the heart attacks if she wasn't plagued by so many other issues. We can possibly keep her 'alive' for a while with machines, but I don't think she would want that."

"She would not want that, Dr. Dawson," Zach replied. "We've discussed this several times. Doesn't she have a DNR on file? Twenty or so years ago when Dr. Gray first told her about the brain tumor and possible outcomes, she told him, 'Doctor, you can't scare me with Heaven. It's too real to me. I've looked forward to it all my life. If a brain tumor gets me there quicker, so be it.' Dr. Dawson, she's in the hands of her loving Lord. Please keep her comfortable until He comes for her. May I sit with her until then?"

CHAPTER 21
Friday, July 26, 2058

On Thursday afternoon, the medical staff moved Kara to a private room on in the hospice center on the second floor. Except for when Sara and Sophie had insisted Zach take a nap on the couch in the room, he sat beside her and held her hand.

Kissing her hand and with tears freely flowing, he began, "Kara, thank you for fifty years of loving me. You are everything I ever wanted in a wife. I certainly married up when I married you. You are kind, gentle, generous, talented, wise, and patient. I have never deserved you.

"I know you were embarrassed a month or so ago when that gal at the supermarket walked up and in awe said, 'You're beautiful!' But you are. You've gotten more beautiful as the years have gone by. Your natural beauty pales when compared to your inner beauty, strength, and grace. What a glorious combination!

"We've shared a lot of experiences. A lot of ups and downs. Definitely more ups than downs. We've gone places and seen things I never dreamed of seeing as a youth. God has directed our steps. Your grace and kindness sparkled wherever we went, whether in a humble village in Cambodia, a chalet in the Alps, or a grand hotel in Warsaw. You've enriched people. We raised two good kids who are both active in ministry. We've been blessed.

"I know the last twenty to thirty years have been a challenge because of your health. But I don't remember you ever complaining. A couple of times you allowed yourself to have a short pity party, but you deserved it. You pushed and pushed yourself when many others would have stayed in bed and moaned. I used to get so frustrated because I could see how tired you were or that you were hurting, and you kept pushing. I really got upset when different ones cried on your shoulder because of their sprung eyebrow, hang nail, or other such thing when I knew you were hurting much more than they could imagine. But you never complained.

"Instead, you praised God through it all. You taught me so much about praise and worship and prayer. Your life of praise has affected so many people. Our church is so much stronger because of your example.

"Honey, I know we had a couple of hard bumps. I've made so many mistakes. I was almost a prodigal who threw it all away. I'm so sorry I ever doubted you. Your love has been so sincere and pure. I am such a better man because of you. You taught me to be more compassionate and sympathetic. I wish I could tell you what's in my heart. Other than the Lord, you are the best thing that ever happened to me! I love you!

"Babe, it's almost time for you to go. Your breathing is getting shallower, and your pulse is getting weaker. I will miss you so much!" Zach sobbed. "I commit you to the care of the King eternal, immortal, invisible, the only wise God. To Him alone be honor and glory for ever and ever. I entrust you to the One who forgave all of our sins, to the One who redeemed us by His blood, and to the One who reconciled us to Christ. I release you, honey, to enjoy all the wonders and beauty of Heaven. I will be there as soon as I can, but God still has something for me to do. Tell Mom and Dad and your parents hello.

"You know, I really don't know what Heaven is like. The Bible talks about mansions, a crystal sea, streets of gold, gates of pearl, and walls of jasper. I hear stories about how Grandma is crocheting table runners for the marriage of the Lamb. Others talk about the fish that Uncle Lloyd is catching in the River of Life. I think that is probably people's fanciful imagination. Or maybe that will take place in the Millennium. I don't know.

"I think Heaven will simply be an eternity of praising and worshiping God. I'm convinced the gates of pearl and streets of gold will all fade away in the glorious splendor emanating from the throne of God. Thank you for teaching me how to praise God in all situations. I will look for you, my love, at the feet of Jesus."

CHAPTER 22
Wednesday, July 31, 2058

Alone in the sanctuary, except for an usher at the rear doors, and dressed in his new charcoal suit with a new bright, paisley silk tie, Zachery Zane Petersen raised his hands in worship as he stood in front of the flower-draped casket. As tears rolled down his cheeks, he thanked the Lord for a life well lived and of the blessing his wife had been to him. He prayed for strength to make it through the time of visitation and then the memorial service that would follow. As he prayed, his daughters Sara and Sophie quietly slipped their hands around his waist and hugged him. He smiled and said, "It's time. Let's do this. Let's celebrate her life!" He then nodded to the usher to open the double doors.

The Prodigal Sister

Warning: This story mentions rape.

CHAPTER 1

Sophie Black enjoyed her perch on the organ bench at First Church. The old Hammond B3 organ sat on its own small riser off to the side of the platform. The view allowed her to see the entire congregation, even those in the balcony. She amused herself by noting the pairing in the youth group. Her husband's nephew, Daniel Black, seemed to have a new girlfriend every month. She wondered how many more girls he would date before he left for college in the fall.

An usher caught Sophie's attention as he quietly slipped up to her mother, whispered in her ear, and then stepped back to allow her to precede him out of the auditorium. A few minutes later Kara Petersen reentered the auditorium accompanied by a shabbily dressed, proxy blonde with full sleeves of brightly colored tattoos. They took seats in the back of the sanctuary. It took Sophie a few minutes to recognize the newcomer.

Sophie glared at the woman sitting next to her mom. It was her older sister Sara. It had been almost five years since Sophie had seen her. She wished she had stayed away. Sophie looked over to the praise singers to see if Moriah had seen her mother. Her niece's pallor and strained expression made her think she had. Sophie clinched her jaw. She couldn't wait until service was over so she could rail against the prodigal sister.

As soon as she could, Sophie made her way back to her mother and sister. Several people had gathered around and were chatting with Sara and her mother. Sophie pushed her way through friends and jerked

Sara by the arm. "We need to talk. Now." She pulled Sara away and dragged her to the empty nursery.

As soon as they were alone, Sophie began, "How dare you to show up now! Look at you. You're an embarrassment to Mom and Dad. What did you come back for? You had better not do anything to stop us from adopting Moriah!"

Sara did not respond but simply turned to leave. Sophie grabbed her and pulled her back into the room. "Hey, we're not done. You can't just show up and act like nothing has happened. Are you pregnant again? Who's the father? Or do you even know?"

"Who died and made you God? You self-righteous..." Sara sneered.

Interrupting, Kara Petersen forced her way through the door. Her piercing glare halted conversation. "Sophie," she said, "that's enough. Half of the church can hear you screaming. You would be more welcoming to a prostitute than you are to your sister."

"Is there a difference?" Sophie replied snarky.

"Sophie, that's enough!" Mrs. Petersen's reply left no room for further retort and conversation.

Turning to Sara, Mrs. Petersen said, "Let's get you home. I put a roast in the crockpot for dinner today. It should be ready when we get home. I'll microwave some potatoes and warm up some green beans."

Before leaving the room, Kara Peterson said quietly but pointedly, "Sophie, you are not welcome until you can treat your sister with more respect. She's our guest. I've raised you better."

When the Blacks got home, Steven Black asked, "What is she doing here? I heard you screaming at her from the foyer. The judge terminated her parental rights almost a year ago. I don't think she can do anything to stop the adoption. Besides, it doesn't look like she can even support herself. I'll call your dad tomorrow and see if I can find out any information."

"I don't know why she's here. I'm so afraid she's going to upset Moriah and try to block the adoption. She not a fit mother. It's not fair to Moriah. It's not fair to us after all that we have invested in my niece. I will not make her see her mom if she doesn't want to. Every time she's come back in the last thirteen years, she's created chaos. This time she was gone for five years without any kind of contact. I get so angry with her!"

CHAPTER 2

It was mid-afternoon before Moriah made it home. She had gone out for pizza with her Sunday school class and their teacher, Kaye Richardson, and her husband Ian. For the last three years—since shortly after Sophie and Steve's marriage—Moriah she had lived solely with them. Before, she had divided the time between Steve and Sophie's house and the parsonage with her grandparents. The Blacks were in the process of adopting her. The adoption should be completed before Moriah's birthday in six months.

The first questions Moriah asked as she set her purse on the entryway table were, "Mom, what is *she* doing her? Do I have to see her?"

"No, dear," Sophie said wrapping her arms around Moriah. "You do not have to see her—unless you want to. In a few months you will legally be our daughter. We couldn't love you any more than we already do. I will do everything I can to protect you from her. She will undoubtedly be gone in a few days. She normally is. She probably came home to get money from Mom and Dad. I don't know why they keep enabling her!"

"Why would I want to see her?" Moriah replied. "She has proven time and time again that I mean nothing to her. Even when she sobered up when I was three and she got an apartment for us, she was no mom. When her doofus of a boyfriend made it clear I was in the way, she shipped me to Mimi's. She chose a first-class loser over me! I don't care if I never see her again."

Sophie's jazzy ringtone interrupted the conversation. She looked at the caller ID. "Hello. What can I do for you, Mother?"

"I'm so glad I caught you before you took you Sunday afternoon nap," Kara Petersen began brightly. "I need you to bring Moriah here so she can see her mom."

"It isn't going to happen! Moriah just asked me if she had to see her, and I told her no. The judge terminated Sara's parental rights months ago. She has no claim on her. Steve and I are her legal guardians. And furthermore, Moriah does not want to see her. Is that plain enough?"

"Sophie, I'm your mother, and I want you to bring her over here."

"And I'm going to be Moriah's mother, and I don't want her around that woman. There hasn't been one time that Sara hasn't cause chaos and left Moriah in tears."

"Sophie, you don't understand. Sara is trying to change."

"Yeah, Mom," Sophie replied. "How many times have I heard that? I didn't believe it then; I don't believe it now. If she changes—really changes, lasting changes—then maybe Moriah will agree to see her. At this point, Moriah wants nothing to do with her—just like Sara didn't want anything to do with Moriah when she was littler. She just had too many guys to sleep with and didn't have time to be bothered with her daughter. Mom, don't let her sob stories fool you. She always was so dramatic."

"Your dad wants to talk to you," Kara said.

"Sophie, please bring Moriah over her so she can see her mother."

"Dad," Sophie replied, "Moriah does not want to see Sara. Sara is not her mother. The judge terminated Sara's parental rights. Steve and I are her guardians. We don't want her around that woman. We don't want Moriah hurt again. We don't want to spend the next two months trying to repair the damage done by Sara leaving her one more time. Moriah can't understand what she did to make her mother hate her; why she isn't good enough for her; why she would choose a druggy ex-con over her. Moriah doesn't want to see her. I'm not making her if she doesn't want to!"

"Sophie, as your pastor, I'm asking you to bring her here."

"Well, Pastor Petersen, you just overstepped your pastoral authority.

I can't do anything about you being my dad, but you are no longer my pastor. Consider this as a request for a letter of transfer for Steve, me, Steve, Jr., and Moriah to the O'Fallon church. Have a nice evening, Reverend. Oh, also consider this my resignation as the music director and Steve's resignation as the Christian ed director."

CHAPTER 3

"Well, when is she coming?" Kara Petersen asked.

"No, she isn't," Pastor Zach Petersen replied. "She said Moriah doesn't want to see Sara. She also said I am no longer their pastor. They submitted verbal resignations as the music director and the Christian ed director. They asked for a letter of transfer to Marcus Tanner's church in O'Fallon."

"She's just upset. She'll come around. She always does."

"I don't know about that. She's pretty defensive about Moriah. I really don't blame her. Sara never has treated Moriah right. She's never displayed any maternal instincts toward her. She always left it up to you and Sophie to care for Moriah. Sophie was the one who always tried to smooth things over when Sara would take off with her latest boyfriend. This is one time when we might have pushed too far."

Pastor Marcus Tanner was waiting for Sophie, Steve, Steve Jr., and Moriah the following Sunday morning in the foyer of Bethel Church. Marcus's daughter grabbed Moriah and led her to the junior high Sunday school class. She quickly introduced her to the other students and made sure Moriah sat next to her when they went to the auditorium for the morning service.

"Good morning, Cuz and family! Welcome to Bethel!" Marcus said, embracing Sophie and shaking Steve's hand. "Zach called earlier in the week and said you might be here this morning. I understand it has something to do with Sara showing up again."

"Thank you for the welcome!" Steve said, shaking Marcus's

hand. "Yes. Things got a little tight with Mom demanding that we take Moriah over to their house so Sara could see her. Moriah wants nothing to do with her. I think that is totally understandable. Dad tried to use his pastoral authority to coerce Sophie to acquiesce. We both thought he was overstepping his position as pastor. I was proud of Sophie for standing her ground. As she said, she can't do anything about him being her father, but she does have a say about who our pastor is, Pastor.

"Anyway," Steve continued, "we really don't want to involve you in what is essentially a family squabble. But considering the situation, it seemed like the wisest choice is to transfer to Bethel, especially if Sara's 'changing' and going to be around for a while. Naturally, we have resigned our responsibilities at First Church. Mom Petersen made it clear that we are not welcome at their house until Sophie can treat Sara like a sister should be treated. Since Sophie's not welcomed at the house, I guess they just expected she would drop Moriah off. It ain't gonna happen! We're just afraid that Sara is going to try to do something to derail our adoption of Moriah. It should be official before her birthday."

"I understand your situation. Do you know how long Sara is going to be around?"

Sophie looked disgusted. "I wish she would leave tomorrow! I know that isn't the Christian attitude, but I have to protect Moriah. From the look of things, Sara is sick. She's extremely thin. Her skin is blotchy. She has a hacky cough. If I know Mom, she will force Sara to go to the doctor. She probably needs to detox too. Mom said she's trying to change. Right! We know how that goes."

"Well, as I said, you are welcome here for as long as you want to be here. You can be as involved as you want. I know both of you are exceptionally talented. I know my wife will want to involve Sophie in music ASAP. We are also looking for a couple to teach the high school class. Would you be interested?" Marcus asked.

"One more question before I go in," Marcus concluded. "Would you like to join us at the Hacienda for dinner? There are always several families from church that show up there. A lot of the time, families from the Collinsville church are there too."

Steve and Sophie enjoyed the morning service. However, it seemed a bit odd. For one thing, Sophie was sitting next to Steve and their son in a pew instead of on the organ bench or standing at the keyboard. The worship was spirited, but the music wasn't quite as polished as at First Church. The sermon was powerful, but not quite as articulate as her dad's. It would take some time to really feel at home in their new church.

CHAPTER 4

Kara was growing more concerned about Sara. Her cough was getting worse. She ate only sparingly. She was running a low-grade fever. She stayed in bed most of the day because she said she didn't feel well enough to get up. Finally, Kara forced Sara to go to the ER.

The doctor diagnosed Sara with double pneumonia, anemia, and two different STDs and admitted her to the hospital. She would be on oxygen, strong antibiotics, and iron for several days as well as a blood transfusion. Afterward the medical team would re-evaluate Sara's condition and decide on any further treatment.

After a week, Sara's lungs were almost clear, and she was breathing on her own. However, she still tested positive for STDs and would remain in the hospital for another round of IV antibiotics.

The two weeks in the hospital gave Sara time to evaluate her life. She despised the person she had become. She had allowed one trauma that wasn't even her fault to dictate her life. Her body lay broken. She was jobless and had no legally marketable skills. She was an embarrassment to her family. Her daughter and sister hated her. Death seemed like a welcome respite.

Sara faced a crossroads. She couldn't continue as she had been. One of her roommates had died from an overdose. Sara knew where she could get the drugs. It would be a painless death. Like her friend, she would simply go to sleep and never wake up. Or Sara could turn back to the God of her childhood.

She wrestled with the decision for days. Finally, on Wednesday afternoon, Sara confessed her sins and, in the quiet of her hospital room, God's Spirit brought freedom and new life. She was reborn. Suddenly she had hope and direction for her life. It would be a struggle, but Sara knew what she wanted to do. She wanted to take the biggest disaster in her life and turn it into something positive to help others.

Kara immediately noticed the difference as she walked into Sara's room. The heavy spirit was gone. Sara's eyes were bright and alive. "What happened?" Kara asked as she embraced her older daughter.

For the next hour Kara and Sara cried, smiled, and rejoiced as Sara told her mother about the change. "Mom, I've been on rock bottom these last two weeks. I'm sick. I'm unemployed. I'm directionless. And I just couldn't continue like that. The only solution I could see was taking the easy way out with an overdose. But I kept thinking about the story for the prodigal son. That well describes me.

"This afternoon, I made my way back to the Father's house. Here, in the quiet of this room, even with my IV lines and attached to monitors, the Lord refilled me with His Spirit. And I feel like He's given me hope and direction for my life. I want to become a counsellor for troubled youth. There's a whole lot you and Dad do not know. I want to take the worse things that have happened to me and make them a positive for someone else. I have hope, Mom. I have peace.

"Remember how Great Grandma Tanner use to say that no life experience is wasted when one is living for God. She said God will use even what we consider the terrible things in our life to help others. I've had a lot of bad things, many because of my bad choices. So, if you and Dad will let me, I want to live with you until I can finish my undergrad degree and find a fulltime position. Of course, I will have to get my master's too."

Tears rolled down Kara's cheeks as she hugged her daughter and marveled at the grace of God. For years she had prayed for this day. Seeing it fulfilled made her realize once again the endless love of God that reaches down to the lowest sinners and elevates them to be heirs with Jesus Christ.

CHAPTER 5
Four years later

Moriah clutched the envelop and rushed to her bedroom. She had waited impatiently for the results of her DNA testing. She deeply loved Aunt Sophie and Uncle Steve, whom she now called Mom and Dad since they adopted her a few years ago. However, the adoption did not replace the deep longing to know who her biological father was. She slit the envelop open and extracted the multi-page report from Kindship, Inc. She quickly scanned the information and then let the paper fall to the floor. The report raised questions she needed answers to.

She picked up her phone. "Sara, this is Moriah. Can I talk to you privately? I got some information today that I do not understand and hope you can explain some things."

"Do your mom and dad know you want to talk to me?" Sara asked. "I know things are much better between us than they used to be, but I don't want to upset them. If they will give you permission to talk to me, then please come on over."

Moriah walked into her grandparents' home and met Sara in the family room. Without preamble, she simply walked over to her biological mother and handed her the DNA report. "NO!" Sara screamed as she read the names and probable relationships. "Is this possible?"

A pale Sara hugged her daughter. "Moriah, I really did not know. Honestly, I didn't know. I think it's time for me to 'fess up to some things." Tears welled up in Sara's eyes. "However, I want your parents and grandparents here when I do. Mom and Dad should be home within the hour; they're making some hospital calls. Call Sophie and Steve and tell them I'm asking them to come over as soon as possible." Tears fell freely from Sara's eyes.

An hour later, Moriah sat between Sophie and Steve on the floral sofa. Zach and Kara Petersen sat on the loveseat beside the fireplace. Sara sat in front of the fireplace in a dining room chair. Tension filled the room. No one looked relaxed, especially Sara who kept twisting her ring. "Uh, thanks for coming," she started. "This is going to be embarrassing and hard."

Taking a deep breath, Sara continued, "I don't think you know, but Moriah sent off a DNA sample to Kindships, Inc. Please don't fault her for wanting to know who her biological father is. It's only natural. She got the results today. However, instead of answering her questions, the report raised questions that she thought only I could answer. However, I didn't even know until I saw the results." Sara let the tears continue to flow freely.

"Before I give you a name, I have to tell you a story. It's not a pretty one. It's one I have never told anyone before. This is hard. Please bear with me.

"First, Dad, I know you always considered me to be a bit rebellious. I really wasn't, but I was always questioning and pushing the envelope. But, nevertheless, I still followed your rules.

"The story took place the spring term of my first year at the university. My roommate was a party animal, but she respected me, and we went our separate ways. However, one night—this is hard! Please don't interrupt—she brought her boyfriend back to our apartment. She had never done that before. They had been drinking and brought some hard stuff in with them.

"Several other people came with them. Two girls and five guys. I knew two or three of the guys from my English class and chatted a few minutes with them. I drank my Diet Coke, and they had their beer and vodka and whatever the others brought. When I got back from the bathroom, I noticed that another guy had showed up. He looked familiar but I couldn't place him. He leered at me and said, 'What's a good Christian girl like you doing here?'

"We all chatted a couple of minutes more while I finished my Coke. By that time, things were getting rather X-rated, and I went to bed. This had never happened before.

"The next morning, I woke up with a horrible headache. I was naked. My pajamas and underwear lay on the floor. There was blood on the sheets. I had severe abdominal pain. I panicked! I could only assume that someone had put something in my Coke when I went to the bathroom and then raped me after I passed out.

"When I saw my roommate, she gave me a sneery grin and said, 'Sounds like you were having fun last night. I know that at least four of the guys enjoyed your wares last night! I hope you're on the pill!' Then she laughed like it was a big joke.

"I was mortified. I had been gang raped! I was angry. I was scared. I was embarrassed. But then a couple of weeks later, I started having morning sickness, and I took a home pregnancy test. It was positive.

"As you know, when the semester was over, I came home. I was just beginning to show. You asked who the father was. I didn't know. How could I? I was knocked out and then raped. I was so humiliated, so scared. I was so embarrassed. And you, Dad, said something about reaping the seeds I had sowed. But it wasn't my fault! But I didn't think you would ever believe that!

"As I began to show more, you all became more and more embarrassed. How could I humiliate you so much? I felt so lost. I felt like God had forsaken me. I mean, how could a loving God allow this to happen to me if He still loved me? Your sanctimonious bigots at church judged me and said cruel things to me. Finally, I stopped going to church. I know, Dad, that you thought it was simply my rebellious nature. But it wasn't. I was hurting, and no one, most of all you, Dad, seemed to understand or care. I just couldn't take the attitudes anymore.

"After Moriah was born, every time I looked at her, I saw the boys in the apartment leering at me and their evil smirks. All the fear and anger and hurt just looped itself in my brain. I wanted to really love my baby, but she was a constant reminder of what happened. The trauma. The pain. The anxiety. I'm so sorry, Moriah! It wasn't your fault! You deserved better!

"Then post-partum depression set in. Physically and mentally, I couldn't handle it. That's when Mom and Sophie had to step in. Sophie couldn't hide her disdain. She didn't try. I felt so horrible, but I couldn't do anything about it.

"Finally, I took off. I took a bus to Milwaukee and spent a few nights with a girl from school. She got me some stuff that made me feel better for a while. But then I needed more and more of the stuff to make me feel good. I still needed the stuff when my savings ran out. The dealer said I could pay with my body. What other choice did I have?

"That was the first time I came home. I wanted to change. I wanted to take care of my baby. But after a couple of weeks, I couldn't take the ridicule and animosity anymore. I stole some money from Mom's purse and started hitchhiking. I didn't care where I went. What difference would it make?

"I came back a couple of times after that. But I couldn't stand the condescending, judgmental attitudes, so I left again. I spent some time in jail for soliciting. That gave me contacts I needed so I could really work the streets when I got out. The tattoos that you all hate so much helped me fit the image and get more work."

Zach and Kara surrounded Sara and held her close. Over and over, they apologized for not being more understanding and supportive. Sara was almost out of control. Deep sobs racked her body. Tears created large wet stains on her blouse.

"I never told you what happened because I didn't think you would believe me," Sara continued. "It was just my rebellious streak; 'You sow to the wind, and you reap a whirlwind.' I was hurting so badly and all you saw was my growing stomach and then my lack of caring for my baby. I knew I was wrong. But I didn't know what else to do. The entire church judged me and found me weighed in the balances and found wanting. But Moriah's biological father sings in the choir every Sunday and is hailed as a pillar of the O'Fallon assembly!"

Shocked and questioning looks passed back and forth from Zach, Kara, Sophie, and Steve. "Who is it?" Kara asked. Sara simply reached down and handed her mother the report. Kara uttered a strained "What?" and then passed the paper on to her husband. He quickly read the names and relationships and then passed it on to Steve and Sophie.

"Well, well, well! Ian Richardson," Steve said. "Way to go cousin! Well, distant cousin—if that. His great grandmother and my great maternal grandfather were cousins. Both were Hodges. We kids always called his grandparents aunt and uncle because they were older and semi-related. His grandparents raised him after a drunk driver killed his parents.

"I understood Ian really liked to party after he left the church. He crushed Aunt Jean and Uncle Tom's hearts. He tried to sample everything he was taught against as a kid. By the time he was a senior in high school, his reputation as a player and dealer was well known. His life spiraled further downhill when he went to university and more debauched opportunities presented themselves. His life took a drastic change eight to ten years ago when he was in the car accident that killed his girlfriend and their baby. The accident wasn't his fault as the other driver ran a stoplight and T-boned them. However, Ian was drunk. She was six months pregnant and drunk. That's when he made things right with God."

"I never put it together until now," Sara said. "When he asked, 'What's a good Christian girl doing at this party?' he must have recognized me from youth camp. I thought he looked familiar back then."

"So, what do we do now?" Moriah asked. "He's married to my favorite Sunday school teacher. They have three kids. I don't want to mess up their family. But he raped my mother; shouldn't he have to pay? Or at least be made aware that he has a daughter he didn't know about?

"But I really don't want anything to do with him. He has always been so condescending to me at church. He's made a few comments about the difference in the color of my eyes and my hair. He asked me one time if I knew who my biological father is. He said it might be one of his relatives."

"Really?" Steve replied. "That's interesting. Several relatives—primarily on that branch of the family—have two different colors of eyes. The deep auburn, curly hair is also a common trait."

Zach turned to Sara and Moriah and asked, "What do you want to happen? If I had a daughter I didn't know about, I would want to know. However, I think Moriah has a definite point that we don't want to cause problems in their marriage. But surely, Kaye knows about his past and that God has forgiven him."

They all looked at each other but said nothing. "Okay, how is this for a suggestion? Steve, why don't you invite Ian and Kaye to your house for a family barbeque? That way it won't seem strange when Kara, Sara, and I show up. I'll call and tell Marcus what's going on. As your and their pastor, I think he needs to be aware of the situation. I'll invite him to the barbeque too.

"After we eat, the kids can play outside while the adults, including you Moriah, simply tell Ian that we got some information that we think he would be interested in and just show him the DNA report. We'll keep it all low keyed and allow him and Kaye to decide how much of the information he wants made public."

CHAPTER 6

Steve had two grills going on his deck. The pork steaks sizzled. The chicken was already on a platter as were the wieners and burgers. Sophie and Kara were setting the corn on the cob, potato salad, and watermelon slices on the table as Ian and Kaye walked through the kitchen and onto the deck, carrying chips, a bowl of fruit, and a German chocolate cake. Sara and Moriah carried green beans and a large green salad. Steve asked his father-in-law to pray, and then everyone began passing the heavily loaded bowls and platters. The conversation included plans for the revival at First Church and the national Youth Congress. Sophie and Steve were taking Moriah to the conference as her graduation present and making several stops along the way.

While the younger kids played on the swing set, the adults went inside. As they found seats in the spacious family room, Zach began, "Ian and Kaye, we invited you here today because Moriah recently received some information that we think you will be interested in. It's a bit shocking. And because of its nature, I asked Marcus and Ruth to join us. I think you know that Marcus is my cousin as well as your pastor. Richard Tanner, Marcus's dad, is by mother's brother." Then Zach passed the DNA report to Ian.

Ian looked at the report with puzzled eyes and then passed it on to Kaye. "I don't understand," he said. "Is this saying that Moriah is *my* child? How can that be? I've never even dated Sara."

"Ian," Sara began, "my first years at the university, I roomed with Darlene Rogers. She was a party animal—God, this is hard! One night she brought her boyfriend back to the apartment, which she had never done before. They had been drinking and brough more alcohol with them. Then more people came. By the time I got back from the restroom, you had completed the group. By the time I finished my Diet Coke, the room was getting steamy! I felt really uncomfortable and went to bed." Tears were falling down Sara's cheeks.

Unable to look at Ian, Sara glanced at Moriah and then looked at the floor. "The next morning, I woke up with a horrible headache. I was nude. My PJs and underwear were scattered in the room." Sobs racked Sara's body as she continued, "My roommate leered at me and said it sounded like I had a fun time the night before. Then like it was a big joke, she said at least four guys had sex with me. Someone had spiked my Coke with some drug that knocked me out.

"I came home and, of course, Dad wanted to know who the father was. I didn't know. I was so afraid. So embarrassed. So angry. I was pregnant, but it wasn't my fault! I was a virgin when I went to bed. Whoever was the first of the four that raped me, took my virginity."

"I had no idea who the father was. I only recognized the guys from my English class. I had no idea who the other guys were that came to the apartment. You looked familiar, Ian, but I didn't know why or how I might know you. And, of course, I didn't know which of the guys raped me.

"I was a lousy mother. I'm ashamed of that. Looking at Moriah just made me remember that night and the horror I felt the next morning. I couldn't take it and finally left. I'm so glad that Sophie and Steve became the parents that Moriah deserves. They and Mom and Dad stepped in when I couldn't. And for as much as I could, I forced memories of that night and events that followed to a small recess in my brain that I locked and threw the key away.

"However, Moriah wanted to know who her biological father is. Unbeknown to any of us, she sent a DNA sample off to Kindships, Inc. for analysis. That's the report that you have in your hands. Moriah read it and had questions that she thought only I could answer. When I saw the report, I called Mom and Dad, Sophie and Steve, and Moriah together and told them about the rape. It was the first time I ever told anyone about it.

"Moriah is seventeen, soon to be eighteen. You do the math. It happened a long time ago. We were different people then. Since then, we both have straightened our lives out and rededicated them to God. Even without knowing who they were, I forgave the men who raped me. From the report, you were one of them, Ian. I forgave you years ago. I had to for my sake. The bitterness, hate, and self-loathing that I carried were too much to bear. I surrendered them to God.

"Ian, I don't want or need anything from you. Moriah and I do not want to do anything that will adversely affect your marriage. What happened between you and me happened a long time ago, before you ever met Kaye. Mom, Dad, Sophie, Steve, Moriah, and I have discussed this situation. We are leaving it totally up to you and Kaye how you respond. You can make a public declaration, or we all can keep it a secret between us.

"I think you should know that when I came home that last time, I was dying. A lot of the time, I wished I were already dead. I had been on the street for five years and had STDs. While in the hospital, I kept thinking about getting drugs and ending it all. However, on the Wednesday of the second week, the Lord came into my room. I felt Him embrace me and tell me He loved me, that there was NOTHING that I could do to diminish His love for me. His love was total and free. With me still hooked up to monitors and IVs, I repented, and God refilled me with His Spirit.

"Then He called me to be a counsellor to help teens navigate life's twists and turns. What was the absolute worst thing that had ever happened to me has become the reason I want to live to help others. Since that day I have finished my undergrad, and I'm almost done with my master's. I'm working full time for Mercy House, a Christian counselling ministry focusing on teenage drug addictions and human trafficking. I love my job! God's been good! My life is good!

"And one of the blessings God has given me is a relationship with Moriah," Sara concluded. "I'm not trying to be her mother; Sophie's doing a fantastic job. I'm more like her crazy aunt. But I'm happy with it. And I think she is too."

✦

CHAPTER 7

Everyone looked at Ian, waiting to see how he would respond. He glanced nervously around the room. Then with his eyes focused on the floor, he replied, "First, I have no memory of the night Sara was talking about. It could easily have happened just the way she described it. Many other nights were similar. My friends and I did things back then that I am totally embarrassed even to think about now. Paul and Stuart often carried ruffies with them. They were probably guys from your English class. The three of us and Dominic Russell sometimes shared women. So, Sara is undoubtedly correct.

"This news is shocking only because of the relationship we all have. I was as honest as I could be with Kaye before we married. She was aware of my sordid life and was willing to bear the consequences. This all happened before I met her. So," Ian continued looking at Kaye, "I don't think this will affect our marriage. Am I right, Kaye?" Kaye squeezed his hand and nodded in agreement.

"Sara and Moriah, all I can say is that I am sorrier than I can begin to express. Thankfully, I'm not the same man I used to be. I was the classic prodigal son. I couldn't wait to throw off the parental restraints—in my case the grandparents' restraints. I indulged in every sin I could find. I was amoral. I am ashamed of my past. But after I hit the bottom— just like in the Gospel of Luke—the Father ran to me and forgave me of all my sins. Now the blood of Jesus has cleansed me. I've been washed clean. I'm a new creature in Christ Jesus…but sometimes sowing wild oats produce a harvest.

"Moriah, I am undoubtedly your father," Ian confessed. "We can do a more comprehensive DNA test if you want. But I'm satisfied with the report you got. I think I even teased you a couple of years ago about you having two different colors of eyes and dark auburn curly hair like several of my relatives. You probably don't know I wear a brown contact in my right eye so it will match the left one. And I think I joked about you being related to me. Of course, I had no idea you actually were.

"You have great parents in Steve and Sophie, Moriah," Ian continued. "They've done a fantastic job in raising you to be a self-confident, God-centered young woman, who is beautiful, talented, and intelligent. You'll be going away to college in the fall, so what kind of relationship do you want with me? If it's okay with Steve and Sophie, I would like to help pay your tuition. I would have wanted to do more if I had known earlier."

"Thanks for the offer on help with my tuition," Moriah began with a chuckle. "I'll accept on behalf of Mom and Dad." Then looking at Ian, she continued, "Honestly, Ian, I don't know how to answer what kind of relationship I want with you. Steve and Sophie are Mom and Dad. They have always been there when I was sick, hurt, or depressed. They provided everything I've needed. They have loved me when no one else seemed to. They have treated me just like I was their biological kid. No offense, but you and Sara were just a sperm and an egg donor.

"Sara and I have had some rocky ground." Moriah continued, looking at Sara. "For a long time, I hated her. I didn't understand why she hated me so. But we've been getting along much better. And now knowing about the gang rape put a lot of things into perspective. I've forgiven her; and she's forgiven me. As she said, she's like my crazy aunt. I like that. Considering everything, I think this is the best relationship we can have. At least I'm happy and contended with it."

Taking a deep breath, Moriah continued, "So I suppose, Ian, that is the kind of relationship I would prefer to have with you. You being an uncle figure to me. But I don't want anything between us to interfere with your marriage and family. If you want to keep our relationship a secret between the ten of us, I'm comfortable with that. I've always considered you a bit condescending and thought you looked down on me because I was born out of wedlock. But I love Kaye! She's a fantastic Sunday school teacher. So, I don't want anything to hurt her, your marriage, or your children."

Since the main players had seemingly said what needed to be said, Zach turned to Marcus and asked if he wanted to add anything. "Well," he began, "I was surprised, shocked, even stunned when Zach called me and told me the results of the DNA test. Because this affects you all and potentially other members of my congregation, he thought I should know. I appreciate that, Zach. Ian and Kaye, I will support whatever decision you guys make about going public with the news.

Looking at Moriah, Marcus said, "I think Moriah shows a great deal of maturity by being willing to conceal paternity so it doesn't embarrass you and your children. No one should hold Sara responsible for being raped. And Ian, you are not the same man you were in college; the blood of Jesus has washed your past clean. Ian, if you admit paternity, the congregation will understand and not hold it against you. So, whatever you guys decided, I'll support." Marcus paused and then with a chuckle said, "However, I personally would hope a relationship would develop between Moriah and Ian so she realizes he is not a pompous, sanctimonious wastrel. But that does not necessarily have to involve revealing the father-daughter relationship."

"I'm not proud of what I've done," Ian responded, "but I am proud of the woman my daughter is becoming. I will gladly admit paternity if we can think of a way to do it without embarrassing Sara, Moriah, Kaye, or our kids. I would prefer that this news is not treated as gossip. I guess that means making an announcement of some kind. Do any of you have suggestions?"

Everyone looked at each other with blank expressions. Finally, Kaye spoke up, "I think Moriah is a super great young lady. Steve and Sophie have raised an amazingly confident woman for all the things she has dealt with in her young life. She was born out of wedlock. She never knew her father. She was abandoned by her mother. Yet her concern is that the news of her parentage does not damage Ian and my marriage or cause undue embarrassment to our kids. Either way you look at it, that's a mature, selfless attitude. I would like to celebrate Moriah. But I don't know what that looks like. And I don't know how to do that without highlighting past mistakes.

"I also think we are overlooking two very important people in our discussion," Kaye continued. "Steve and Sophie, what are your reactions to this revelation? Are you willing to allow Ian and our family to have a relationship with Moriah? Even though you are not her birth parents, you chose to love her and to care for her and to make her your own. No one can or wants to change that. So, are you willing to let Ian be a part of Moriah's life? If so, how do you see him—us— playing that role?"

Steve and Sophie looked at each other and then at Moriah and then the Petersens and Sara. Sophie took a deep breath and then said, "We love Moriah. That will never change. The good thing about love is that it is expandable and designed to be inclusive. For example, when Steve Jr. was born, the love I felt for him did not diminish the love I have for Moriah. So, I have no problem with the Richardsons and Moriah developing a relationship. As Moriah has suggested, perhaps an uncle/niece type situation would be best.

"Moriah is leaving for college at the end of the summer. We have already begun planning—shut your ears, Moriah—a surprise going away party. What if the party included Ian and Sara becoming 'God parents'—for the lack of a better term—to Moriah? If you are comfortable with the idea, we can say that DNA testing has revealed that Ian and Sara are Moriah's birth parents and that no one was aware of this until recently. I don't think it's appropriate or necessary to elaborate beyond that. No one else needs to know about the gang rape aspect of Moriah's conception. That would put the emphasis on Ian and Sara instead of Moriah."

"Steve, are you okay with this idea?" Sophie asked.

"Yeah. I like the 'God parent' idea," Steve replied, "although I think I would prefer a better term. And I totally agree we should place the emphasis on Ian and Sara recognizing their shared parentage of Moriah and their new relationship to her. This so reminds me of Romans 8:28. How could anyone ever imagine that Ian's debauched life and Sara's rape would result in something good?"

"Dad," Sophie said, "can you help Steve and me devise a program to go along with this idea? Perhaps a take-off of a baby dedication where the parents promise to raise the child in the ways of God."

CHAPTER 8

Those invited to Moriah's going away party filled the fellowship hall of Bethel Church. Silver and navy, the colors of George M. Sponsler Academy, decorated the walls. The academy is a church-sponsored liberal arts college, with a heavy emphasis on missions and ministry. It would be Moriah's future home for the next four years in Gresham, Oregon.

Tables containing a buffet of finger foods, assorted salads, sliced fruit, and mini desserts zig-zagged in the middle of the room. Scattered around the room were drink stations with bottled water, fruit punch, and canned pop.

Also attending the party was Parker Martin, who captured Moriah's attention at the national youth congress a month ago in Indianapolis. He would also be going to Sponsler Academy, but he would be attending the graduate school and working toward his master's in Christian Ministry degree. The constant texting, video chats, and smiles attested that the duo had formed a tight bond in just a few weeks. Steve and Sophie wondered how much studying Moriah and Parker would do at the college.

Zach Petersen acted as master of ceremonies, got everyone's attention, and called Steve, Sophie, and Moriah to stand beside him. "It's been said that you choose your friends, but you are stuck with the family that you are born into. That is true most of the time. However, from time to time, a person is blessed to be adopted by parents who *choose* to love him or her and who *purposely* pick that child to be theirs forever. Steve and Sophie found Moriah and welcomed her into their family through adoption. The theological aspects of adoptions elevate it to a special kind of love.

"Moriah loves Steve and Sophie. That is evident in so many ways. And while Moriah is confident in the love and security that Steve and Sophie give her, she was curious about her parentage. She knew her birth mother, but she had no idea who her birth father was. So, unknown to any of us, Moriah sent a sample of her DNA off to Kindships, Inc. to find out more about her biological parents.

"The results of those tests came back a few weeks ago and shocked all of us. Let me say we are all sinners saved by the grace of God. Even we who have grown up in church were sinners in need of salvation. One thing that intrigues me about God is how He can take the bad and horrible things of life and turn them into something miraculously beautiful.

"The DNA tests revealed one of these beautiful things. As I said the test results were startling. We had absolutely no idea who Moriah's father is. He was as shocked by the test results as Moriah's extended family is.

"However, her biological parents are so proud of the young woman that Moriah is becoming. As a biased grandfather, I can say she is beautiful, intelligent, gifted, and so much more. Let me also say that her biological mother was unable to take care of Moriah because of emotional and health issues. And of course, her father did not know he had a wonderful daughter. So now that the truth is known, these biological parents want to publicly acknowledge their daughter and pledge to support her, to honor her, and to champion her for the Christian lady she is.

"Sara Petersen and Ian Richardson, will you please step forward and join hands with Moriah and Steve and Sophie." Shocked chatter spread across the room as Sara and Ian joined hands with the others.

"Ian and Sara, do you acknowledge that Moriah is your biological daughter and a gift from God? Do you recognize Steve and Sophie as Moriah's parents and pledge to uphold their parental rights? Do you promise to support Moriah spiritually, emotionally, mentally, and—as God provides—even financially? Do you promise to consistently pray for Moriah and keep her before the throne of God? Do you promise to respect her as a woman of God and to give her wise counsel if she should ask? If the need should arise, do you promise to provide a safe haven for Moriah?

Ian and Sara answered yes to each question. Then Zach said, "Let's pray."

"Father, we so love You and your family. We recognize that we all have sinned and fallen short of Your glory. We're so thankful that You can take our shattered lives and mistakes and make them into something that is beautiful and gives glory to You. I thank you that you provided loving parents for Moriah when her biological parents were unable to keep her. And now that Moriah's biological parentage is known, we thank You for their love and concern for Moriah. As we all adjust to these new relationships and as Moriah leaves for college, be with each of us. Lead us. Guide us. Protect us. And help us to grow in grace and the knowledge of You. In Jesus' name we pray.

"Ian and Sara, this was not on the schedule, but do either of you have anything you wish to say?"

Ian was the first to speak up. "Although by grandparents raised me in church, I rejected God's love and became a prodigal. I'm embarrassed and ashamed of things I did. Through the years I was a hellion and hurt many people as I sought my own pleasure. But I'm thankful I'm not the man I used to be. God has forgiven me. He has reconciled me to Christ. He has redeemed my past by His blood. And as a testament of His grace, He's given me a beautiful daughter. She already has a dad, so I'm going to be the best uncle that I can to this amazing young lady."

Ian turned at looked at Sara. She swallowed and said, "I am one of the ones Ian hurt but not necessarily intentionally. I did not know him then. But a few years ago, I forgave him even though I did not know his identity. The load of hate and bitterness that I carried was too heavy to bear. I gave it all to Jesus. For a long time, I was emotionally, mentally, and physically unable to take care of Moriah. But now God has allowed me to develop a relationship with her that I do not deserve and never expected. God has forgiven the guilt and hate I carried. I've reconciled with my daughter. As Ian said, my past has been redeemed. I agree that Moriah has amazing parents. I will never be her mother. But I'm thankful I can be her crazy aunt."

Few eyes remained dry as the guests embraced Ian, Sara, Steve, Sophie, and Moriah.

CHAPTER 9
Five years later

Mom, I wish Parker and I had just eloped! It would be so much cheaper, quicker, and easier. I thought once I had chosen the bridesmaids, their dresses, my dress, and the songs for the ceremony, I had made my decisions. Dad read me the riot act the other night. He was asking about some details about the reception—he was working on the budget and spreadsheet—and I didn't care whether we had potatoes-au-gratin, scalloped potatoes, or rice pilaf. What difference does it make?" Moriah asked as she and Sophie were making bird seed packets guests would throw outside at the newlyweds following the reception. Sara and Kaye were on the other side of the table rolling the cutlery in napkins and tying them with a bow.

"Well, I doubt anyone except your dad would remember on your tenth anniversary if you even had a dinner," Sophie answered. "I'm glad we are nearing the end. The wedding is only four days away. I was a bit worried about how your grandpa would feel about sharing the officiating with Marcus. He was fine. He was even going to suggest involving Marcus as he was your pastor for several years."

"By the way, Mom," Moriah said, "Uncle Richard Tanner has agreed to pray just before the pronouncement. Dad asked him to use the same prayer he first prayed at your wedding. He also used it at each of his grandkids' weddings. It's the line, "May every realistic expectancy of which they have dreamed come to pass according to Thy divine will for their lives," that gets me. 'Realistic expectancy' sound so much like Uncle Richard. And it's fitting, because sometimes my dreams are not realistic and probably do not conform to God's will for my life with

Parker.

"Dad and I also went over the seating chart for the ceremony," Moriah continued. "Aunt Sara, you and Uncle Ian and Aunt Kaye will sit on the second pew on the left, right behind Mom—and Dad, after he walks me down the aisle. I want everyone to know that I love my biological parents regardless of the hows or whys. I am who I am because of your DNA. But I'm also who I am because I have two loving parents who adopted me and love me and trained me when my real parents couldn't care for me."

Sara wiped tears from her eyes. She had a lot of regrets, but she had so much more to be thankful for. She loved Moriah; she was blessed they had a healthy relationship. She loved her job; she was glad she could make a real difference in the lives of her clients. She loved her life. She marveled at how God had taken her broken, messed up life and turned it around. The worst event in her life led to even more devastating decisions to where suicide seemed to be her only escape. But that was when the love of the sovereign Lord enfolded her. That was when she realized He had allowed the terrible things to happen to her because He could take the shattered pieces and make her life beautiful, fulfilling, and one that glorifies Him.

The
Prodigal Father

CHAPTER 1

My name is Jeremy Tanner. This is my story.

Let me briefly introduce three others that will interrupt me from time to time to share their insight to what happened. Paul Tanner is my father and the former pastor of this church. Yes, his older brother is the Reverend Richard S. Tanner, the bishop of the churches in the state for our denomination. Francis Faith Cooksey Tanner is my mother. Michael Abbott leads the altar workers team for Christ Church.

The praise team had just ended its first set of praise choruses. The presence of God electrified the service at Christ Church. We were off to a wonderful start. As my assistant stood to walk to the pulpit to receive the morning's tithes and offerings, I got a signal in my earpiece from the head usher. "Pastor," he said, "we've got a problem. You may…" The rest of the message was drowned out by the sound of the main sanctuary doors being shoved open and a man screaming, "Jesus, I need you!" as he ran to the altar area and fell on his face before the pulpit, sobs wracking his body.

The man was tall, gaunt, and stooped—whether by emotional or physical condition, I could not tell. He wore a worn navy suit and gold tie. His salt and pepper hair partially covered his ears, and his grey beard needed a trim.

I didn't know what to do, and all eyes were on me for direction. I nodded to the ushers and altar team leader to escort the man to the prayer room. The assistant continued to the pulpit to make the announcements and receive the offering. As the ushers raised the man to his feet, he raised his faced and looked at me. I knew him!

CHAPTER 2
Jeremy

I went through the motions of preaching my sermon and gave the expected altar call that rainy April morning. However, for me the service ended when I saw the man's face.

He was my father. He was the former pastor of this church. I had not seen him in fifteen years. The last time was when he stood behind the pulpit, impeccably dressed in a charcoal suit and a red silk tie. He looked over the congregation with a troubled stare. Then he looked at my mother on the front row where she always sat with Kent, my two-year-old son, beside her. He then turned to me in the chair beside his on the platform. He cleared his throat, hesitated, and then said, "This is my last service here as your pastor. For the last seventeen years, I have taught you biblical principles upon which to base your life. However, for the past three years, I have been living a lie. I have not lived what I preached. I have been unfaithful to God, to my wife, and to you. I know you will not understand, but please forgive me." He turned and walked off the platform and out the side door of the sanctuary near his office. That was the last time I saw him until he ran to the altar, although I tried many times to reach out to him.

That morning I watched the color drain from Mom's face. I could see he had taken her by complete surprise. She was in shock. She was having trouble comprehending what he had said. As he left the building, she hurried after him. However, she was too late. He got in his black SUV and drove off, not once looking back.

The congregation sat in shocked silence. No one moved. No one said anything. Finally, I walked to the pulpit. Embarrassed, I picked up the mic and said, "I am as stunned as you. I do not know what is going on. I ask that you pray for my father. It's evident he's having a personal spiritual crisis. I ask you to pray for my mother, our family, and each other. I'm not sure what we are facing in the next few weeks and months."

I continued, "I guess we have to accept this as my father's resignation, effective immediately. I am asking the trustees and other board members to meet next Wednesday to begin the search for a new pastor." I asked the congregation to stand, gave the benediction, dismissed the congregation, and quickly folded my arms around my mother.

The news and developments in the ensuing weeks were devastating. The calls and emails I received as the news spread kept repeating the same two words: *unbelievable* and *shocking*. A well-respected member of the city clergy, Dad had embezzled forty thousand dollars from the church treasury. He had cleaned out half of his and my mother's savings. He had been having several affairs, including one with his neighbor, my mother's best friend and church secretary. Her husband and family were hurt and angry but decided to try to repair their marriage. I did not blame either of them. I was simply trying to understand the totality of the situation as it affected our family and the church—and even the community at large.

As young as I was, I was fortunate that the board recommended that I be elected lead pastor. The vote was overwhelmingly positive. I was really humbled by the support. It could have so easily gone the other direction. I requested that my mother to be allowed to remain in the church parsonage.

CHAPTER 3
Jeremy

I know the Bible teaches we should forgive those that wrong us and turn the other cheek. I preach and teach that. But I was having trouble dealing with it then. It's easier to preach it than to live it. For fifteen years I've had to deal with the destruction my dad inflicted on this congregation. I saw my siblings struggle to maintain their spiritual equilibrium. I watched Michael and Sue trying to repair their damaged marriage. Sue struggled with forgiving herself for being so gullible to fall for my dad's lies and for the wounds she inflicted on Michael and her three teenagers. I witnessed the financial hardship his stealing caused; for one thing the entire church staff had to take a 20 percent pay cut. I saw how his betrayal caused so many to lose trust in the ministry. A third of the congregation stopped coming. Some just completely quit attending church while others became members of congregations in neighboring communities.

And now, Dad wanted God to forgive him? And he expected the congregation to receive him as the father received the prodigal son? I don't think so! Besides, at least a half of the congregation is new since he left. I really didn't know what he expected.

I trusted him. He was my father. He was my pastor. He was my mentor. He instilled in me great biblical truths for which I will always be thankful. I idolized him. But he hurt me so deeply! When he confessed fifteen years ago, it was the same as stabbing me with his hunting knife. I was so blindsided and devastated. So humiliated! I was crushed! And how could I help to pick up the pieces of the hundreds of shattered lives?

How do you explain such a confession to your children? You teach them to respect the ministry and to submit to spiritual leadership. You teach them to love their grandparents. But what if it is their grandfather/pastor that destroyed their foundation of faith? I watched my children and my siblings' children struggle spiritually and emotionally. So many times, I've wanted to do I don't know what to him for the trauma they've endured.

"Father God," I prayed, "please forgive me because right now I can't forgive him. Please help me to be Christ-like and love him as You love me. Without Your help, I can't. I want him to be saved, but I wish he had gone to another church in another state." My feelings were so raw right then.

CHAPTER 4
Francis

Irecognized Paul as he ran past me that night. I no longer sat on the front pew but on the center aisle midway back. The hurt and anger that I thought I had dealt with the past several years came rushing back. It's as if every scar was ripped open, and I realized I still had so much anger—well, really hate—that oozed from the wounds.

First, I had been embarrassed and humiliated by his public confession. I was so naïve and blind. If there were signs, I chose to overlook them. I felt so betrayed by him and Sue, my best friend.

Second, he destroyed me financially. He stole our money and left me facing bankruptcy. I had no income of my own. I had been the dutiful pastor's wife for the past twenty-five years. I know how to dress appropriately and decorate on a tight budget. I know how to organize a ladies' ministry, run the Sunday school, play the organ, and to sing. I've even reluctantly directed a choir a time or two. I've counselled hundreds of women through their own spiritual struggles and marital problems. I had all the answers until I didn't even know the questions.

How do you describe being a pastor's wife on a secular resume? I had never used my education degree except for a couple of years when we first married. I had no marketable skills. I never needed to. We were in this together until death do us part. Except, neither of us died, although I wished I had.

Third, he stole my identity. I was the pastor's wife of one of the larger churches in the county. I was respected as a community leader and active in several civic organizations in town. I was the Ladies

Ministries leader for the churches in our state. I was lauded for my creativity and leadership. Fifteen years later, I still hang my head in public. The groups I belonged to no longer reach out to me. I am a shadow of who I was.

Fourth, he destroyed by family. Tim was a junior in college when Paul pulled his stunt. Tim worshiped his father, but his father destroyed him. Tim became rebellious and refused to go to church where once was so active. He began hanging out with the wrong crowd. He was drunk when his car slammed into the back of the semi, instantly killing him and his college roommate.

I confess I was a bitter, old woman. And I hated that I still loved Paul. God, have mercy on me!

CHAPTER 5
Michael

When Pastor nodded at me to take the bum back to the prayer room, I was excited that a new person wanted to give his heart to God. But then as he stood, I recognized who he was. Suddenly I hated my responsibility. I felt so hypocritical! How could I pray and ask God to forgive this man when I had so much animosity toward him myself?

He wrecked my home. Sure, Sue and I are together, but it's different than before. She swore the relationship was only emotional, not physical. But I had a tough time believing it. I tried to forgive her for the kids' sake. I knew she was remorseful. She has tried so hard to regain my trust.

Her affair with Pastor devastated our three children. Bethany had always been the one living on the edge. She was always asking, "Why can't I _______?" She was the one I always worried about. After the news of the situation broke, she became more openly rebellious. If Sue tried to correct her or pull her back, Bethany would shut her down with, "Oh, but shacking up with the preacher is okay?" It really wasn't too surprising when Bethany got pregnant her first year in college.

Kaitlyn has always been more dedicated to Christ than Bethany. She had always looked up to her mom and was so shattered by the disappointment. Her faith was shaken. But somehow, she found shelter and security in Jesus and grew stronger in her consecration. Nevertheless, the rip in her and Sue's relationship has never been mended.

Evan was away at University of the Great Lakes when the sordid details broke about his mom and his former pastor. Thankfully, he had already found his niche at his new church and in its college/career group. The news shook him up. However, his counselling with his new pastor helped him to see that we all are humans saved only by the grace of God. No one is above temptation and falling into sin. And as humans, we make mistakes. If we repent, God forgives. And if God forgives, then we should too.

So now the man who caused all of this was standing beside me. Before I could pray with Paul, I had to empty myself before God. As I exalted His holiness and purity and confessed my own sinfulness, I realized I was to blame for much of the tension at home. My attitude hadn't been right. After fifteen years, I still had so much anger and resentment that it affected my relationship with Sue and the kids...and God. As I truly confessed and repented before God, the hardness of my heart slowly melted. A thankfulness I hadn't experienced in a long time filled me. I am so grateful for the love of God that washed me clean and forgave my sins. Uncommon praise to my Redeemer filled me. And as I looked at Paul, God gave me a love for the man I once despised.

Paul's repentance seemed genuine. I noticed his hesitancy when I put my hand on his shoulder to escort him back to the prayer room. As soon as we stepped into the room, he stopped and, with tears streaming down his face, he told me he was so sorry for what happened between him and Sue. He took all the blame. He said nothing physical happened sexually because Sue wouldn't let it. Weeping, he was a broken man.

CHAPTER 6
Paul

I didn't mean to interrupt the service that morning. I intended to wait in the parking lot until Jeremy gave the invitation and then slip down to the altar. However, my heart was so heavy; I felt so much conviction. I knew I could no longer carry the weight of my sins. There was only one way to find release. I couldn't wait.

I was always embarrassed when something like that happened when I was pastoring. It normally happened when a drunk got under conviction and stumbled into the church. My son handled it the way I taught him to. However, expressions of surprise, disbelief, and embarrassment—even fear—flickered across his face when he recognized me.

I'm so totally ashamed of what I'd done. I have no excuse. Everything I had, including my relationship with God, I threw away. Just like the prodigal son, I purposely ran from the Father's house. I don't know what I was even thinking. I thought I had it all worked out when I walked out. I had planned for months. I deceived myself; I won't even blame the devil.

I sold insurance when Francis and I started the church in Mehlville and did quite well. That was years and miles away before we were elected to Christ Church. I had maintained my insurance license through the years because the field interested me. Because of that, when I contacted Bill at my old office, he offered me a job. So, when I left fifteen years ago, I drove the 200 miles back to Mehlville to a furnished apartment I had rented online. I again started selling insurance later that week in a neighboring county.

Without going into detail, I told Bill I had left the ministry, and then I desperately tried to keep my past in the past. I knew I had done wrong, but I really didn't want to bring more reproach on the ministry than I already had. Wanting to make a break from the former life, I began to hang out with the men in the office. Soon I was trying new things.

The adage that sin is a slippery slope is so true. Once I tossed aside what had been personal disciplines, sin dragged me further and faster down the dark path than I ever intended to go. I don't know what I was thinking when I was planning my "escape from bondage." But I certainly wasn't expecting to do the things I did. My curiosity and weaknesses just led me further and further astray. I was shackled by sin.

I'm not going to glorify what I did. I'll just say I never intended to become so enslaved and bound. Addictions almost destroyed my career. My health was broken. I had to move to a studio apartment. I was already on the bottom when the doctor told me I was HIV-positive. I assumed it was from an infected needle but maybe not. Who knows?

The doctor's report made me face reality. I knew I had two alternatives. I could take my life and end my pain, or I could make the prodigal's trip back to the Father's house. I began trying to clean my life up and prayed for the first time in years. I felt hope, but the devil told me I had gone too far from God and that I would always be his slave. He said I had hurt my family and they would never forgive me. Nevertheless, something kept pulling me back to the church. I know it was God. I thought I had to return to the place where I had thrown everything away.

That morning, it startled me to realize Michael Abbott was the one leading me back to the prayer room. I had to apologize to him before I could confess to God. I was so sorry and embarrassed I had wrecked his and Sue's family. Of course, God knew my desire to return to Him.

I was so humbled as the men in the prayer room gathered around me. A few knew me from years ago. Some were new to the church. However, each one manifested a love and compassion for me that I did not deserve. I confessed my sins and felt the surge of the Holy Ghost as the Lord renewed His Spirit within me.

Forgiveness is a wonderful feeling. I was so overwhelmed by the mercy of our Father. I had willingly turned my back on Him, but His love covered and still covers my sin. The weight was lifted. I felt clean! Joy filled me as I began to speak in the heavenly language once again. I know experientially that no drug, sex, or anything else the world has to offer can give you the high that the joy of the Lord can. Truly, all that thrills my soul is Jesus!

I knew I'd made things right with God. I felt His peace. I had renewed my vows. He had restored me. I was forgiven, redeemed, and reconciled. But I also was afraid of what I would find beyond the prayer room door.

CHAPTER 7
Jeremy

The altar service had ended, and many people had left for home or the restaurants before my dad, Michael, and the other men left the prayer room. I could tell by the shouting and hallelujahs coming from the prayer room that Dad had repented and had been refilled with the Spirit.

I was happy, even excited, for the spiritual change. It was something I had prayed about for years. However, I didn't know how to react on a personal level. Was this change sincere, or was he just trying to fool us all?

I forced myself to walk over to him and embraced him in a tight hug. It felt weird. "Welcome home, Dad! It's been a mighty long time. Come home with me. Spend the night. The guest room is ready. I would like for you to meet your new grandchildren."

He didn't know how to respond. His face showed how conflicted he was. He finally agreed, but I could tell he was embarrassed.

However, I saw him straighten up and look around. Then he walked purposefully to my mom. I didn't know she was still at the church. She flinched as she saw him walking toward her. I didn't know what to expect.

He sat beside her. She stiffened—her back becoming ramrod straight. He began talking to her as his shoulders shook and tears fell down his cheeks. She glared at me and pulled away from him. Rebuffed, he stood stooped shouldered and sorrowfully walked back to me.

In the meantime, I told Anna that Dad was staying with us that night. I could tell that would not have been her choice, but what else could I do?

CHAPTER 8
Francis

I fumbled with the keys as I unlocked the door to my apartment. I really don't remember leaving the church that morning. That had been one rollercoaster day! My emotions had been all over the place. I didn't know what I was supposed to think or feel. The man I prayed for for so long had finally repented. I saw the transforming joy of the Lord on his face. Yet the past years of anxiety and anger and brokenness filled me with bile. I wanted to throw up. I wanted to forgive him. I knew I needed to forgive him. But right then I couldn't. I didn't want him to talk to me. I didn't want him to touch me. I didn't want to see him.

I felt hollow. I went to church and went through the motions of being a born-again Christian. I still taught the ladies Bible study on Tuesday nights in the chapel. But it had been so long since I have just basked in the presence of the Almighty. I knew what the problem was. Bitterness had consumed me for fifteen years. I can't describe what happened to me the night Paul confessed to the church and walked out. My life stopped.

I have tried to be strong and support Jeremy as he dealt with the fallout. I tried to say the right things and do what was expected of me. But it has been all an act. I tried to hide the excruciating pain. I had to laugh inwardly when friends told me I was handling the situation so well. If they only knew.

CHAPTER 9
Paul

I made it through that first night at Jeremy's. It was awkward. I purposely stayed in the guest room until the kids had left for school. Jeremy and I had talked long into the night. He wanted to know what happened, why did I do what I did. I had been asking myself that question for the past several weeks.

The easy answer is burnout. The stress of the local church, activities in the district, and oversea missions travel all took their emotional and physical toll. But, if I'm truthful, the problem was much deeper. I liked the accolades and calls to preach conferences. To be in demand stroked my ego. I began to believe my own PR. I allowed my ego to expand and grow. And as I began to believe more in myself, I began to let prayer slip away. If I'm honest, the lack of prayer was really my downfall. That's where it began. Heartfelt prayer would have kept my ego in check. It would have kept me balanced. It would have kept me focused on His kingdom. But I let it slide.

Francis usually went with me on my missions trips but not always if she had a ladies seminar scheduled or the kids needed her for something. The stress of travel and the pressure of the meetings were exhausting. I was always so worn out when I would board for the flight home. On one transatlantic flight, it just seemed logical to open the small bottle of wine that came with the meal to help me unwind and relax for the long trip. Then another time I missed my flight from Africa and had to layover in Paris till noon the next day. I clicked on the TV to find something to relax me. Instead, a porn channel popped up and my curiosity took over. Another time a woman came over and sat at my table as I was eating dinner at the airport. I justified my actions because I was so tired. It was almost like a reward for my sacrifice for missions.

What happened as a one-time fluke became a pattern. I was glad when Francis found excuses not to accompany me.

CHAPTER TEN

Jeremy

Two years quickly passed since Dad prayed through and recommitted his life to Christ. My prodigal father had come home. He lived in Melhville and continued to sell insurance and annuities. His health was improving. At least he wasn't as gaunt as he was.

He attended a small church in the country near his condo. I had feared he would want to attend our church. That wouldn't be good on several levels. Besides the feelings from the older members who remember "the good old days," I didn't want Mom to have to deal with the awkwardness. And to be truthful, I didn't want to deal with it either.

I believe his repentance was sincere. Two of the older district board members told me they received letters of apology from Dad for his— what do I call it? —his mess up/affairs/backsliding/fall from grace. I admired him humbling himself to apologize. His young pastor, who knows his past, asked him to teach some Bible studies. If God opens more doors for him to minister, I hope he walks through them.

I still struggled with my own reactions. I tried to be open, loving, forgiving. The hurt ran deep. I still saw the pain on Mom's face. I thought of all the time my children and their cousins were cheated out of having a loving grandfather. It was harder to preach about forgiveness because I felt so convicted when I did.

I prayed for a clean heart. But I had so many bad memories of the deceit, thievery, betrayal, wounded hearts, and broken spirits. Would it have better if he had just overdosed, and I could bury the past? My thoughts condemned me. I wanted to do better.

CHAPTER ELEVEN
Francis

The years continued to fly by. I documented my life in my journal. This is what I wrote on the fourth anniversary of Paul's repentance:

It's been a while since I journaled my thoughts. Four years ago this morning is when Paul ran to the altar at church. My life hasn't really changed. The only thing that keeps me sane is the stability and security of my job at the bank. In the past twelve years, I've completed my degree in finance and received several promotions. I feel more confident as a person. I'm more social, not hiding like I was. However, Paul is never too far from my mind.

I wish he had died! Then I wouldn't have to keep riding this emotional rollercoaster. My friend Fiona attends the same rural church as Paul, and she mentions him from time to time. He taught a Bible study series on the Epistles that was well received. He always was an excellent teacher.

I wish I could forget the past. It haunts me. It smothers me, and I gasp for air. Paul keeps his distance and never bothers me. However, he sends me cards for my birthday and special occasions. It's what he used to do. I resent it! We're still legally married, although separated by a vast gulf that I cannot span. I want to forgive him. I assume that desire is progress. When he first apologized, I refused to listen. I just wished he had died and had never showed up at church.

I know my attitude has made things difficult for Jeremy and his family. The kids would like to invite their grandpa to their birthday celebrations and holiday dinners. But the couple of times we both showed up, the tension was unbearable, and Paul left early. He now mails his gifts and comes around only when he knows I will not be there.

It feels so unfair. It's like I'm punishing the grandkids for something they're not responsible for. I wish I could erase the past twenty years.

CHAPTER TWELVE
Paul

God has been good to me in the seven years since I gave my heart back to Him. Seven is God's perfect number. I have paid back the money I had stolen from the church. I sent a cashier's check to Jeremy to give to Francis for half of the money I took from our savings account. (I wanted him to know what I had done and to ensure she got the check.)

I just left Jeremy's. I took Roseleigh out for lunch for her birthday. Then we went to the mall so she could pick out her gift. She wanted a new dress for the national youth convention in Atlanta that is coming up in a couple of months. She's a beautiful young lady. Tall and regal. She normally wears her hip-length blonde hair in a French braid or an elegant chignon. She so talented! Smart. She reminds me of her grandmother.

I wish I could make things right with Francis. I've tried to apologize several times. She won't listen to me. She won't even look at me if she can help it. I know I did wrong. I admitted it…to God and to her. He's forgiven me, but she refuses. I have quit going to birthday celebrations or family dinners for holidays, because it makes Francis so uncomfortable. I messed up; so now I pay the price.

Otherwise, life is good. I teach a men's Bible study on Thursday nights and sometimes the pastor has me preach when he goes out of town. The advantage in going to a home missions work is that the members do not know my history.

I cut back my hours at the office. I probably should completely retire, but I don't know what I would do. I work to keep busy. I've done well selling insurance and my 401K looks great. I live frugally and save so I won't have any financial worries when I do finally retire.

I also began writing like I used to. I'm writing short commentaries on the Pauline epistles and offered them for use in our Global Missions Bible schools. Teaching in the overseas Bible schools was something I always enjoyed before my fall. So far, the books have been well received. And that too keeps me busy.

On a bright note, my health has greatly improved. I think it really goes back to the night I was prayed for at the district camp meeting. The young guest minister often operated in the gifts of the Spirit. He made a call for anyone suffering with a chronic illness to come forward for prayer. No one knew about my HIV diagnosis. I hadn't even told Jeremy or any other members of the family. I guess I was too embarrassed to. Anyway, I went to the front for prayer. I didn't feel a bolt of lightning going through my body as some have testified to as he prayed for me. I really didn't feel anything supernatural. But I clung to the promise in James 5:15, "And the prayer of faith shall save the sick, and the Lord shall raise him up; and if he have committed sins, they shall be forgiven him." I believed it! And now the doctor says I'm HIV free. Praise God!

CHAPTER THIRTEEN
Francis

Ten years ago today is when Paul disturbed the Sunday morning service at Christ Church. This is what I wrote in my journal this morning.

Dear Journal, time is passing by so quickly. Kyle, Jeremy's youngest, will soon be graduating from the University of Kansas. Yes, he's a Jayhawk. I would have preferred that he was a Mizzou Tiger, but he preferred the architecture program at KU.

As the songwriter said, "Time is filled with swift transition. Naught of earth unmoved can stand. Build your hopes on things eternal. Hold to God's unchanging hand." I'm a happy grandma, because through all the difficulties of life, Kyle has maintained a close walk with the Lord. Instead of letting dorm life lead to drinking and drugs, he's started a Bible study group in his dorm. Ten of his friends regularly attend the church in Lawrence, Kansas, with him. I'm glad he's getting his master's degree in architecture, but I really think he's feeling a call to ministry, just like his dad and grandpa.

For the past year, the Lord had been talking to me about Paul and forgiveness. He said since He forgave Paul, shouldn't I do the same? I should. I know the blood of Christ was shed to atone for sin—even Paul's. Paul has repeatedly asked for my forgiveness. I know he is sorry. But clinging to the hurt and anger has been such a part of my life that I don't know how to let them go. But I know I must unless bitterness destroys me. The bitterness has affected not only my relationship with God but also with my family. If I know Paul will be at Jeremy's for dinner or a family celebration, I stay away. I'm the one who's missing out. In reality, I'm punishing myself by holding on to my anger.

The other day I read a quotation by C. R. Strahan that said, "Forgiveness has nothing to do with absolving a criminal of his crime. It has everything to do with relieving oneself of the burden of being a victim—letting go of the pain and transforming oneself from victim to survivor."[1] I'm tired of the pain of being the victim. I want to move on. I'm realizing that forgiveness is more for the offended than the offender. If I want true freedom, then I must let go of the past. I must look to the future.

As it is now, the future looks bleak and lonely. I look at my contemporaries with their spouses and envy their closeness. Several friends who lost their spouse have remarried and seem so happy. I miss the closeness that Paul and I had. Could I forgive him to the point that we could have that again?

---

1. C. R. Strahan, Forgiveness Quotes (3457 quotes) (good-reads.com)

CHAPTER FOURTEEN

Jeremy

Mom shocked me when she suggested celebrating Dad's seventieth birthday in September. While I had prayed for reconciliation for the two of them, I hadn't seen any softening on her part until then. It was miraculous! She seemed so determined to hold onto her bitterness. Dad had been a part of our family life since he repented fifteen years ago, but Mom had always stayed away if she knew he would be there. Because of her suggestion, I proposed that Anna and I host a family dinner for all the siblings and grandchildren, and she join us. She readily agreed. Surprise, surprise!

Unfortunately, a phone call from Dad's pastor interrupted my conversation with Mom. Dad had had a stroke and was in the hospital in Mehlville. I told Mom. She wanted to go with me to see him. Thank You, Lord!

When we arrived at the hospital, we hurried to ER as they were still waiting for a room in the main hospital. Dad was paralyzed on his left side. He was alert but his speech was slurred. He was shocked to see Mom with me but gave her a lopsided grin as she reached to hug him. I was amazed at the transformation. It was truly a miracle of grace.

The doctor returned and said they would have a room available in about an hour. He confirmed that Dad had a stroke and that his left side was paralyzed. He held out hope that the paralysis would be temporary and stated that Dad would be transferred to a rehab center in Mehlville by the end of the week.

The doctor went to see another patient, and Mom asked for some private time with Dad. Startled by the request, I stumbled out of the room and went to the cafeteria.

CHAPTER FIFTEEN

Francis

Seeing Paul lying in bed, so helpless and needy, my heart went out to him. The bitterness I had carried for so long just vanished. I know it was the work of the Holy Spirit who had been prodding me for over a year. I was overwhelmed by love for Paul. When I leaned over to kiss him, he used his good arm to hug me. The tears in his eyes and his twisted smile said he forgave me.

I asked Jeremy to give us some time by ourselves. I don't know who was more shocked, Jeremy or Paul. Jeremy left, and I couldn't hold back the tears. The years of hurt and remorse were washed away as I cried and apologized to Paul. Paul tried to respond but his speech was hampered by the paralysis. But as his tears joined with mine, our hearts knitted together.

Mehlville was 200 miles from my home. I was still Paul's wife. I was determined that I would take care of him. The doctor gave us hope of at least partial recovery, although he said it might take a lot of rehab. I wanted to be there for that. The only way to do that was for him to be transported to the rehabilitation center near the church. It was within walking distance from my home.

CHAPTER SIXTEEN

Jeremy

Mom surprised me again. She wanted Dad transferred to the rehab center near our church. She stated she was still his wife and would take care of him. She was willing to take family leave from her job if necessary.

I did not see this coming! I prayed for years to see this, but I was beyond belief. God had done so much more than I had faith for.

It took a few days to get Dad transferred, and Mom refused to leave with me. Instead, we got her a room at the Holiday Inn Express. I also rented her a car so she could go back and forth to the hospital and then have transportation to follow the ambulance when Dad was moved to the rehab hospital.

The response to his stroke and Mom and Dad's reconciliation has been surprising. Those that see them together know they are witnessing a miracle. Only the grace of God could allow Mom to empty her soul of her bitterness. Several of Dad's minister friends have driven miles to see him.

Just like his and Mom's reconciliation, Dad's rehab was miraculous. Highly motivated, Dad really pushed himself to achieve his goals. His physical therapist was fantastic. He knew just how far to push Dad and when to draw him back. I expected the physical therapy, but I didn't expect the occupational therapy. But Dad had to learn how to button his shirt, pull up his socks, slip on his pants with his left side incapacitated. These are things I didn't even consider when the doctor mentioned rehab. Dad really did well. Every day he seemed to regain motion and muscle mass. And Mom rarely left his side. They were so cute together.

The biggest surprise to me was how the church rallied around Mom and Dad. The congregation opened their hearts to them. Several women voluntarily formed a rotation to clean Mom's house since she spent so much time at the rehab center. Men volunteered to make the house accessible for Dad when the therapist released him to go home and to make some other repairs. Even now, I simply stand amazed at how God has orchestrated everything.

CHAPTER SEVENTEEN

Jeremy

Grandma used to say that God would be as gentle as possible to teach us the life lessons we need to learn but firm enough to get the job done. She also said that no life experience is ever wasted. She said that sometimes God puts us in situations so our experience can benefit someone else down life's road. Grandma was a wise lady.

I confess, I really had a challenging time letting go of the past. For years I ached when I would look over the congregation and see the different ones hurting because of Dad's failure. I wrapped myself in righteous robes of self-pity to disguise my bitterness. I wasn't as overt as Mom after Dad repented, but I really wasn't as forgiving as I should have been. It took the innocence of my kids and their open love for Dad to teach me what I needed to do. Then it took the grace of God for me to accept that the blood of the spotless Lamb of God had washed Dad's past clean and buried it in the sea of His forgetfulness. Realizing God had erased the guilt from Dad's life forced me to repent of my attitude. I couldn't expect God to forgive my wrongs if I was unwilling to truly forgive Dad.

It's been a struggle for me. The betrayal was so heavy. The pain was so deep. But now I can honestly say that I've forgiven my dad. Some things will never be the same. For instance, he will not be my mentor or counsellor. He will not be the one I fall back on if an emergency arises in the church. I will not ask him to counsel any parishioners.

However, he is my dad. He has a special place in my heart that only he can fill.

When Dad stood and confessed his sin so many years ago, I didn't think anything could be worse or that any good would ever come from this. Boy, was I wrong! Things did get worse, much worse as more details of the situation became known. But as I now look back over almost thirty years, I see how God has used this for good. The congregation was severely shaken but survived the damaging winds. It is larger and stronger than it's ever been. Individuals that tended to rely on the pastor to see them through crises have learned to look to Jesus and have grown in their faith.

The most profound result is the lessons I've learned about forgiveness, redemption, and reconciliation. It was so easy to preach and teach forgiveness when life was good, and I was so idealistic—even naïve. But then I realized how difficult it is to forgive someone who hurt you—or hurt the ones you love as family members or congregants— as Dad did. I'm much more understanding and compassionate with people who struggle to overcome their own hurts now. I've also learned the necessity of forgiving myself. In many ways my hatred for my dad was as bad as his sins. I had to recognize it, repent for it, and allow God's love and mercy to wash me clean.

I've also realized that forgiveness leads to reconciliation. Reconciliation brings unity to any situation. Love now grows where hate flourished because the offended parties reconciled.

And perhaps the most amazing thing—this is coming from someone raised in church from infancy—is realizing God takes the shattered pieces of lives and broken dreams and redeems them and then forges something glorious and beautiful from the ruins. I've seen this all my life as I have seen sinners repent and God transform their lives. However, to witness it in my own life and the lives of my family is really astounding! If I ever had any doubts about God's ability to do the miraculous, the last thirty years is abundant proof He can and He does.

I often thought of my father as the prodigal who had returned home. I didn't leave the Father's house, but I was so wrong. I acted my part, while inside I was broken. I was confused. Bitterness and strife filled me. But God took the pieces of my tattered, storm-tossed life and made something beautiful. I marvel at how God has taken the very worse experiences of my life and redeemed them to make me a better man, a better husband and father, and a better pastor.

I finally understand what it means to be forgiven, redeemed, and reconciled.

And that's my story. Thank you, Mom, Dad, and Michael for helping me tell it.